Delta Rogue
Seal Team Phantom Series
Book 3

By Elle Boon
elleboon@yahoo.com

Dedication

I'd like to dedicate this book to the men and women who serve and protect our country in any form, from the military, to the police, to the firemen and firewomen, to the medical workers, and beyond. Also, to the loved ones of those who serve and protect us. Thank you so much for your sacrifices.

Love and Hugs,

Elle

Chapter One

Hailey Ashley looked at the lock on her apartment door, and then at the computer screen again. Ever since the man she'd called friend and team member Dex, had betrayed their team, she'd been living in a state of fear. A game of hide and seek and waiting, until he decided to come and take her out. The other guys were big bad SEALs, while she was the only woman in the group who he would consider an easy target. Until a few weeks ago, she was pretty confident she was as badass as they were. Now, she wasn't so sure. Hell, Blake Anderson was one of the toughest men she knew, and he'd been drugged by the asshole, and taken hostage.

A shudder worked its way through her at the image of the other man lying in the hospital bed. Luckily for him he had JoJo, another SEAL member and his lover. Both men were so in love, she sometimes envied their closeness. "I'm freaking pathetic," she groaned to the empty room.

Thinking back, she wondered how they'd missed the fact Dex had been working for another faction. They all lived in the Steinem apartment building, or at least they had, and hung out regularly. Now, she wasn't sure where Dex was, or Maddox Lopez for that matter. When Dex had shown his true colors and allowed Blake to be kidnapped, then tried to take Alexa Gordon in order to trade her to some unknown person, all so he could make a quick buck, he'd betrayed them all. She was the only one out of the team who'd kept a separate apartment in another location, or at least she thought she was. Now, she questioned everything she'd thought she'd known.

The ringing of her landline startled her, but she let it go to voicemail. More than likely, the same person was calling again. "I don't know anything," she said aloud even though she was alone. Somehow a computerized voice would call her at all hours, demanding answers to questions she didn't have. Her job on the team was not glamorous, or even dangerous. She blended, or if the target was female, then she became the friend and confidante. Hailey drew the line at sleeping with a target.

Tired of staring at the walls, and waiting around to be killed, she unfolded her legs from the sitting position. In a pair of black leggings and a tank top that read *Shut the Fuck up*, she slipped on a pair of tennis shoes, then grabbed her backpack. After making sure her gun was safely inside, she headed toward the door. For weeks she'd hid in her home, only going out to get groceries in broad daylight like a coward. She hadn't seen any of the men she'd gotten used to seeing on a daily basis, the ones she'd called friends. For three years, she lived and worked and had no other friends in South Dakota, thanks to her job. Well, she was not going to sit around and mope, or fret anymore.

Mind made up, she unlocked the deadbolts one at a time, then taking a deep breath, stepped into the hall. The quietness was alarming, but she reassured herself it was normal. She turned back around and relocked the door, then with a press of a button, engaged the security system on her keychain. She may be ready to get out, but she wasn't stupid.

When she didn't encounter a soul in the elevator or the lobby, she exhaled a deep breath. One obstacle down, several more to go. Keeping her head up, and her mind alert, Hailey continued to head toward where she kept her Ducati Monster 696. With her keys palmed, she pulled the helmet off the handle bars, strapped it on, then straddled the bike. The sound of the engine roaring to life made her feel alive for the first time in weeks.

She leaned forward over the gas tank, maneuvering out of the parking spot and headed out of the garage. The sound of a vehicle coming up behind her, set off alarms in her overly tired brain. While she waited for the bar to go up, she looked behind herself and saw a blacked out sedan coming up the ramp. Without a second thought, she eased around the guard rail, and left before whoever was in the vehicle could get within shooting distance. Her fight or flight instinct took over before she could think twice, choosing to run as fast as she could.

The sun going down blazed a bright orange and yellow trail as she gunned the engine, putting much wanted space between her and the vehicle. Swerving between traffic, she tried to picture the license plate, and cursed herself for not paying closer attention. If Mad, or one of the other guys had been there, they'd have made sure to get details, or more than likely, they'd have stayed and confronted whoever was in the vehicle.

As the miles passed, she finally let herself cry for the first time. Tears rolled down her cheeks, and dried from the wind while she drove. Her stomach ached from lack of food, making her decision to get out of the apartment apparent. Another loop up the winding road and she promised herself she'd head back to town for dinner. At the very top, she saw a small roadside area and decided to stop to watch the sunset. With nobody else on the road, the need to take advantage of the perfect moment was too hard to ignore. She hated the thought of heading back to Ohio to her family with her tail between her legs. Sure, they'd hug her and tell her they loved her, but afterward, she would never hear the end of the 'I told you so's', or even worse, 'that girls aren't cut out for that line of work' speeches. No matter how much better of a shot she was than her brothers and cousins, or the fact she could kick their asses in hand to hand, it all came back to the fact, her family believed a woman's place was in the home, taking care of the kids.

The sound of her tires rolling over the gravel echoed around her. She stopped the bike and sat up, cracking her back from being bent over for so long. Taking off the helmet, she shook out her hair, and sat for a few minutes. Pushing the kickstand down, she hopped off and went to stand near the edge of the cliff off to the side. The sound of wildlife like a symphony. Going home shouldn't feel like a prison sentence, dammit.

With a resigned sigh, she turned back toward where she'd left her bike.

Headlights coming up the road highlighted the area, making her scramble to reach the Ducati before they got to where she'd parked. With her heart in her throat, Hailey came to a hard realization, she wasn't going to make it as the large truck pulled in behind her motorcycle. She slipped her backpack off, grabbed her gun out, and trained it on the large man exiting.

Maddox, aka Mad Lopez, rounded the front of his Dodge Ram looking way too good for Hailey's mindset. Dressed in a pair of jeans that molded to his muscular thighs, and a tight white T-shirt, she felt her mouth go dry.

"Nice night for a ride, Hales." Maddox's deep rumble had all her girlie parts standing up and taking notice.

She tilted her head, but didn't lower her weapon. "Why are you here, Mad?"

He shrugged his massive shoulders making her want to run her fingers over his muscles. How the man could keep his white shirts pristine, she had no clue. As the seconds turned to a minute she began to fidget, but refused to say another word.

Taking a step closer to her bike, her thought was to get on it and leave him standing on the side of the road. His dark eyes gleamed as if he already figured out her plans, and was two steps ahead of her.

The sound of another approaching vehicle made Hailey tense. "What the fuck? I swear to all that is holy this is usually a deserted stretch of road at this time of night." No sooner had the words left her mouth, than a spray of bullets pinged the ground in front of her. Maddox shocked her as he sprinted toward her, throwing his body in front of hers, then rolling them both away from their vehicles.

Hailey held her breath, the jarring of the fall somewhat cushioned as she rolled with the man who held her securely in his arms. The closer they got to the edge of the cliff, the more she began to struggle.

"Dammit don't fucking fight me. Those bullets are not fake, Hellion," he grunted.

She almost felt bad, knowing he was taking the brunt of their fall. His nickname for her had always made her smile, yet now she wanted to knee him in the nuts. Since they'd left the hospital, she'd been all alone, thinking about her future. Or wondering when she was going to be taken out. Not once had any of the men she'd been working with had the decency to call and check on her. Of course she understood JoJo and Blake's reasoning, but Maddox was supposed to be her friend. Hell, she thought he cared a little more than that.

Their rolling came to a stop a few feet into the timber with her lying beneath him. Looking up into his dark eyes, she couldn't help but be mesmerized. His lashes were longer than most women, and his unblinking stare made you think he truly could see inside your soul. Only the man was heartless. He'd told her time and time again he didn't do love and forever. She'd told him she didn't do one nighters. They'd come to an agreement that they would be friends and nothing more. However, that didn't mean she didn't fantasize about him on the daily, or nightly.

"Keep looking at me like that and I'll say screw the men pursuing you and fuck you right where you are." Maddox traced a finger along her jaw.

His words made her flinch. Trying for a nonchalance she didn't feel, she smirked. "I was just thinking how incredibly unfair it was you had such girlie lashes, while us women had to put mascara on to achieve the same affect. Now, if you'd get your big ass off me, we should probably be seeing if the fucks who were shooting at *you* are still up there." She gave a hard shove to his chest.

He bent his head a little closer. "Little liar. That's okay though. I'll let you get by with it for now." He shoved up onto his knees. "The vehicle is gone already." Maddox stood, holding his hand out.

Hailey pretended not to notice and scrambled up, standing beside Maddox. At five foot six to his little over six feet, she felt small, especially since he was well over two hundred pounds of pure muscle, and wasn't afraid to show it. "What makes you so sure they aren't parked and waiting for us to come back up?"

Maddox shrugged. "I heard the vehicle as it raced away when several other cars came by. I'm assuming they were hoping to catch you alone."

She narrowed her eyes. "Or, you led them here, or they were following you. Nobody knew I was coming here, not even me, big guy."

A muscle ticked in his jaw. Score one for her.

"Hales, don't push me, okay. I was just coming by to check on you when I saw you fly out of the garage on your little bike. I noticed an SUV following you, but with your *driving*, you lost them. I didn't realize we'd picked up another tail. I'm thinking if we check your bike out, we'd find a tracker on it. Want to test my theory?"

He made it sound like her driving was not up to par, which was absurd. The thought someone had tampered with her Ducati had her hurrying up the hill.

"Slow down, and check your surroundings. Dammit, Hellion, you trying to get yourself killed or what?" Maddox's fingers bit into her arm.

Taking a deep breath she ignored his touch and what it did to her body. "Fine, I'm slowing down, but I want to test your theory." Plus, her backpack and gun had fallen when she'd literally been knocked off her feet as the shooting had begun.

A quick sweep of the area near her bike showed they were alone. She could hear Maddox cursing beneath his breath, but she walked a few more feet toward the sleek bike. Not ten feet away from her Ducati, an explosion knocked her off her feet, sending her flying backward. Again she found herself being covered by Maddox as motorcycle parts flew by them.

"Sonofafuckingbitch," Maddox bit out.

She held onto his shirt with both hands, rolling with him as he took them further away from the fire. Hailey didn't feel any pain until their bodies stopped rolling. A trickle of wetness dripped into her eye. "Oh, god. I never cry, yet I've done it twice today," she whimpered.

Maddox brushed the hair away from her face. "You're going to be okay. Stay calm, Hellion."

Her teeth began to chatter and her body shook. "My bike is gone."

He repeated the same words again as a wave of pain washed over her.

"Don't go to sleep on me, Hales."

"I told the guys you were not into guys. Tired, Mad." Her eyes felt too heavy to keep open, and even though she wanted to stare into his gorgeous face, she let them close having memorized every facet of the man in the last year they'd worked together. JoJo and Blake had teased her mercilessly, saying they were sure he played for their team.

"I most definitely don't swing that way, Hellion," Maddox murmured.

Hailey tried to smile, but the last thought she had was she wished she'd had a chance to find out for sure which team Maddox Lopez played for.

Maddox swore in several languages as Hailey went limp beneath him. The cut above her brow gushed too much blood, making him worry she was going to bleed out on him.

"I need a medic here, stat," he yelled through the line in his ear.

"Man, you're undercover." Mike Royce's voice held a tinge of humor.

"Hailey is fucking bleeding out man. Cut the fucking jokes and get me some help." Maddox gave him their location while he put pressure against the wound. Protocol be damned, he wasn't going to let the woman who had come to mean more to him than she should die on his watch, and politics be damned.

"Shit man, you need to keep calm. Where is the Ice Man?" The tone of Royce's voice had dropped to monotone. Not one Maddox liked to hear aimed at him.

Throwing caution to the wind, he asked again. "You making the call or am I?"

"Two minutes out. What's the story?" All business, Royce didn't say another word.

Staring down, Maddox made up his mind quickly. "Everything stays the same. Whoever blew her bike up was probably working with the ones we are after. If Dex is still alive, he's our line to the assholes. I'm sure they think Hailey and I are weak links since we worked closely with the fuck. More so Hailey since I'm new to the team. We got eyes on Blake and JoJo?" He kept his eyes and ears trained on the road, knowing the assassins could come back at any time. Hell, if it were him, he'd already have come back on foot and have a bead on both their heads.

Royce grunted, which was saying a lot for the other operative. The sound of sirens getting louder pulled his attention away from what he'd do, and on what he needed to do. He could no longer afford to keep hiding behind a façade of SEAL, when the threat was now moved up. Maddox wouldn't allow another woman he cared about to be killed in the line of duty, when he could prevent it. "I'm taking Hailey and myself out of the Steinem Building."

He pulled the earpiece out and stuffed it into his pocket before the ambulance came to a stop followed by the firetruck. A plausible excuse for a perfectly good motorcycle blowing up didn't come readily to his mind, making him realize he was in too deep with the woman.

"What's going on?" the first responder asked, taking in the scene.

Maddox didn't move away as the man and a woman approached with medical equipment. "My fiancée and I stopped here to take in the view, when a vehicle roared past. She and I were walking back toward her bike when I dropped my phone. I stopped to pick it up, but Hailey kept walking. The next thing I know I hear an explosion. Hailey screamed, and I ran to where she landed, throwing my body over hers and rolled to get us away from the falling debris." Maddox took a deep breath, and let it out slowly.

"Sir, we need you to move so we can check her out." The female medic edged around him. "Do you need medical assistance as well?" she asked.

The woman would probably freak if she saw how many scars he had. Instead of answering he shook his head, moving back a little to give them room.

Hailey moaned. "Maddox?"

"I'm here, Hellion." He grabbed her hand as she lifted it in the air, moving into her line of sight. "Lay still while the good medical peeps take a look at you."

"Medical Peeps?" Hailey snorted. "I thought I was the one who hit their head."

Maddox relaxed once he heard Hailey talking and watched as she was strapped onto a stretcher. They stopped the blood flowing from her head, and began the walk back to the ambulance. He glanced at what was left of her Ducati, and warred with going with Hailey, and staying to collect evidence.

"You coming with us to get checked out?" The female asked.

Shit! "I'll follow." He pointed at his vehicle. "Don't want to leave my truck on the side of the road." Half-truths were his specialty. Hell, he was CIA, they practically trained you in the art form of telling what the person wanted or needed to be told, spinning it to where it was believable. His job was to protect the country from terrorists, and the latest threat was from someone on the inside.

"We'll let the ER know to expect you."

He met the too wise gaze of Hailey Ashley, and gave a slight nod of his head. If the cops showed up, one with any sort of training, they would probably find a few stray bullets that would be unexplained, but Maddox wouldn't own up to any of them.

He made sure he had Hailey's bag and gun secured in his possession, before following the flashing lights of the ambulance. The small device was literally burning a hole in his pocket. Shifting his leg, he pulled it out and put it back into his ear. "I'm enroute to the hospital to get checked out, and make sure Hales is okay. You want to hack the computers and clear the way for me. Also, see if there are any hits on the attempt on us today."

Silence met his demands, but he didn't have to wait long before Royce would give him feedback. The ride to the hospital wouldn't take too long, and he hoped like hell the other man at least worked his computer skills to smooth over parts for him.

"Your cover is solid for the medical shit. As for any hits on the girl, or you the SEAL, there's some chatter, but nothing too firm. I'll keep my ears open. You do the same, dick," Royce growled.

"Yeah, I know you love me. Didn't mean to shut you out, but couldn't have you bitching in my ear like an ex-wife or anything." Maddox signaled to follow the ambulance, noticing a familiar vehicle a few cars back. "I got me a tail. Charcoal Tahoe with smoked out windows. I don't see a license plate. He's at the corner of Grant and Ackerman. Can you pull up any cameras in the area?"

The sound of Royce's fingers flying over the keyboard filled the air.

"Got em. There looks like three men inside. Or at least three large figures. One looks like your friend Dex from what I can tell through the camera at the stop light. Dumbasses don't know who they're fucking with," Royce laughed.

Maddox came to a stop near the ER opening, looking behind him. "Are they still following me?"

Royce chuckled. "The light is frozen on red. You got a few extra minutes."

Shaking his head, Maddox parked in the first open spot he could find, then hurried to the bay area he'd seen the ambulance go in, uncaring civilians weren't allowed. He had a badge, one he would pull out if the need arose.

"I owe you one, man." He muttered.

"I'd say your first born, but if they're anything like you, forget it. Alright, they are on the move. I'll watch them through cameras as long as I can, and let you know if there's anything you need to know. Keep me abreast on Hailey's condition," Royce said with a touch of warmth.

His appearance had several paramedics looking his way, but none tried to stop him, making him shake his head. At six foot tall, over two hundred and twenty pounds of solid muscle, most people found him a bit intimidating, especially with his dark looks and bald head.

"Figured you'd be right behind us, but not *right* behind us." The male paramedic who'd shown up on the scene raised his brows as they lifted Hailey down from the back of the ambulance.

Maddox shrugged. "What can I say? I couldn't stand the thought of my girl hurt."

Hailey's eyes widened. "I'm glad you're here, Mad."

"His name is Mad?" The woman asked, pushing the gurney with Hailey on it.

"Maddox Lopez, but my friends call me Mad." He grinned as she looked down at Hailey and winked.

"Well, that is a much better reason than what I was thinking."

"Your friends are circling the hospital," Royce spoke into his ear.

Maddox was used to multitasking. His eyes took in the somewhat busy ER, while he listened to Royce keep him up-to-date on the men following him and Hailey.

Damn! He might need backup. He also should maybe ask for the people's name who'd come to Hailey's rescue, then shook his head. They were probably used to small talk. Maddox, ignored the pang of doubt, and kept the smile on his face.

Once Hailey was pushed inside the small triage room, he went along and kept a close watch. He'd fucked up by not anticipating the attack earlier, which could have cost him and Hailey their lives. Maddox didn't make the same mistake twice.

"You've got that look I've seen before. Right before someone is about to go down." Hailey raised her hand up and mimicked shooting a gun.

The nurse working on getting her vitals laughed, thinking Hailey was making a joke, but Maddox and Hailey knew she was telling the truth.

"Hmm, I can think of all kinds of things I could say, but I don't want to make you blush." His words had the desired effect. Easing the tension from Hailey's body, and making the nurse in the room laugh.

Chapter Two

Hailey nearly groaned out loud at Maddox's words. He'd turned what she'd said into something dirty, and damned if all her female parts didn't stand up and say hallelujah. The man was sex on two thick legs, with what she was sure was an impressive package in between. However, not once in the last year and a half had he so much as made a comment that he was interested in her. For fucksake, she'd begun to think he was gay. Not that she had anything against gay men. Her two best friends were JoJo and Blake, who were in a very committed relationship. They were also Navy SEALs, while she was Navy, she wasn't part of the elite group. Not because she couldn't hang with the big boys, but because they didn't allow women in. Instead she was in Navy Intelligence, and was damn good at her job.

"If you could just sew me up, I'd like to get out of here." Hailey blew out a breath.

The nurse snorted. "Hun, I'm afraid it don't work like that. The doctor will have to look you over, and then make his decisions. More than likely, you'll be staying the night. You took a pretty nasty hit, and may have a concussion."

Well, duh, Hailey could've told her that. "I've had a concussion before. I know what to do and what not to do. Believe me, I will be fine."

Maddox and the pretty nurse shared a look. In that instance, she wanted to rip the blonde woman's tits off. Yep, she was so screwed.

"Listen, Hellion, we will wait for the doc, and then make some decisions." Maddox's big palm settled on her thigh.

Her mouth went dry, but she found herself agreeing to his words. The nurse, whose name she couldn't remember nodded then left them.

"I can't stay the night in the hospital, Mad. I'll be a sitting duck for whoever tried to kill me. I need to call my superior...JoJo and Blake need to be told," she began, only to stop as his head descended, blocking out the overhead light.

"Stop worrying. I won't let anyone hurt you."

She opened her mouth to protest, then sucked in a stunned breath when he covered it with his. The ease with which he took control, making her forget where they were, was crazy and wonderful. She'd never had anyone kiss her the way Maddox did. He didn't just move his lips over hers, but nibbled on each one of her lips, then licked along the roof of her mouth, slid his tongue along hers, dueling for supremacy. The act of kissing became a form of lovemaking, and Hailey knew the man would be just as good, if not better when it came down to sex.

Her fingers clutched at his shirt, holding him close. All thoughts of danger, and men out to kill her flew from her mind.

The sound of the door opening had Maddox pulling from her, and facing the door, putting his body between the bed and the intruder.

"Hello, my name is Dr. Mills." The doctor came in holding an electronic pad followed by the nurse.

Hailey licked her lips, still tasting Maddox on them. She couldn't seem to get any words to form. Luckily, Maddox was able to regroup. His warm palm reached for her hand.

"My name is Maddox Lopez, and this is my fiancée Hailey Ashley." As Maddox recited his story of what happened she was able to collect her thoughts. Hearing him call her his fiancée stunned her. She knew it was only so he could get into her room, but her treacherous heart beat faster. In the last eighteen months she'd fallen a little in love with the man.

"Well, let me take a look and we'll go from there."

Dr. Mills came over, his cool hands assessing. Once he finished, he looked down and smiled. "Well, I will agree that you probably do have a concussion, although your eyes are dilating better than one would think for someone who was knocked unconscious. Let's get your cut glued up, and if you have someone who can stay with you, then I'll agree to allow you to go home. I have a feeling you'd prefer that, or you'd leave against medical advice anyhow." White/grey eyebrows raised in question.

Hailey gave a half laugh. "I would prefer to go home."

"I'll be there, and can guarantee she won't be left alone," Maddox promised.

Her heart began to beat faster for a whole new reason. In all the time she'd known the man, they'd never been alone without one of the others.

Dr. Mills took care of the gash, then asked a few more questions, made some notes, and then left. As they waited for her discharge papers, Hailey wondered what they were going to tell their superior. Heck, she wasn't sure what they could say.

"We need to call this in. Blake and JoJo need to be on the lookout." Blake had already been injured and almost killed. She knew without a doubt, JoJo would be devastated if he lost his lover, or vice versa.

"I've already taken care of it." Maddox waived away her concern.

Angry at his easy dismissal, and heavy handedness, she swung her legs over the side of the bed. A slight nauseous feeling had her gripping the edge like a life preserver in the middle of an ocean. She fought the sickness down, hoping he didn't notice. Her wish was futile as he bent, coming up close and personal, his midnight dark eyes taking in everything about her at once.

"Don't be so damn stubborn, Hales. You and I both know whoever is out to kill you, are probably after the entire team. I made the call on the way here while I followed the ambulance. You'd have done the same if roles were reversed." He ran the back of his fingers down her cheek, making it hard for her to stay mad.

She swallowed, happy the contents of her stomach no longer threatened to come back up. "You're right," she agreed grudgingly.

"That hurt, didn't it?" he asked with a grin.

The bright white teeth and full upper lip on his handsome face should have looked feminine, but nothing on Maddox Lopez was girlie. "Only a little."

They were interrupted before she could do something stupid, like lean forward and reassure herself his lips were as soft as they looked, by the nurse with her discharge papers. Maddox stood up, the large bulge in the front of his jeans caught her eyes. He winked when she met his gaze, a knowing gleam lit his features, making her blush. Damn the man, and his ability to make her feel like a teenage girl.

Two could play that game. When she got him on her home turf, Hailey planned to see just how much Maddox Lopez was able to take before he cried mercy. Either that, or did what they truly wanted, and that was break his iron control.

Maddox watched Hailey's entire demeanor change, and without a doubt, knew he was in for a wild ride. He'd known within twenty-four hours of meeting the woman she was trouble, in a good way. It had taken his complete focus to resist the urge to fuck her on any and all available surfaces. Hell, who was he kidding, he didn't need a surface to do the deed. Not with her. His mind had conjured up scenarios where he'd strip her of all her clothes, or to just the bare necessities. Free his cock, and pound into her. With her lean, muscular build, she would be a perfect partner to help him lift and slam her back down on him, over and over again, without the need for any type of place to lay down, or lean against. Yeah, he was a total pervert, and he didn't mind admitting it. His right hand had become his best friend since he'd met one Hailey Ashley. Stroking himself to images of her were like second nature.

Shit! He needed to get his mind off of what he wanted to do, or he'd be walking around with the largest erection he had no chance in hiding, and nobody in the hospital could miss.

They walked back outside to where he'd left his truck, the thought of the assassins still tailing them had him reaching into his pocket. Surreptitiously, he pulled the earpiece out. With the tap of his finger, he had it reactivated.

"Motherfucker, I swear to fucking all that is holy, I will kick your ass if you shut me down again, got me?" Mike Royce swore into his ear.

"Damn, this parking lot is fuller than when I pulled in. Let me check my truck out before we get in," Maddox instructed, figuring his partner had kept eyes on the vehicle while he'd been inside with Hailey.

"I should let you get in and play Russian roulette asshole. However, I, unlike you, am a gentleman. The little lady looks like she could faint at any moment. The truck is clear, and your tail is waiting around the block. I'm in position to help you out with the latter." Glee tinged his best friend's voice.

He made quick work of looking all around the truck, making sure it appeared he was truly checking it out. "Looks clear. Let's get you in and on our way. I don't like standing out here. Makes me feel like a target is on my back."

"Nah, I don't see anyone with a gun pointed at you." Royce's tone had gone serious.

Maddox hated having to speak so that Hailey might assume it was to her, when in actuality it was for the man in his ear. Never had a job conflicted him more.

"Can we get some fast food? I'm actually starving." Hailey's stomach rumbled loudly at her words.

He made sure she was in before rounding the truck and getting in himself, chuckling at the sound of her groan. "Hey, it's normal to get hungry, luv."

Backing out of the small parking spot, he looked over to see her arms crossed over her midsection. Damn bucket seats. If he'd had a bench seat, he could have pulled her next to him.

"Whatever, big boy. I don't hear your stomach making any noises." Her eyes dared him to say something stupid.

At the first stoplight, he checked his rearview mirror. Mike Royce was a crazy son of a bitch, and if Maddox knew his partner, he was more than likely already looking for a way to take the other vehicle out. Or, had already figured it out and was waiting for his opportunity.

Figuring it was safer if he stayed in the busier area, he made a few turns, until he found a restaurant that had a drive thru they both liked.

His truck was far from standard, with more upgrades than met the eye. Unless they launched a grenade, he figured they had a pretty good chance at whatever was thrown at them. Of course, it would be better if they didn't have to face anything at the moment.

"You are clear for takeoff. I repeat. Clear for takeoff," Mike said a little winded.

Unable to think of a way to ask what happened, Maddox nodded. "Good."

"What's good?" Hailey asked.

He shook his head, then pulled forward as it was their turn to get their order from the window. Fuck! He and Mike were going to have to come up with a code or some shit.

"Do you mind if I eat my fries in your truck? Seriously! I feel like my stomach is eating my backbone." Hailey dug into the bag.

He looked at her trim figure, and imagined her naked, and eating her out. With a shake of his head, he pulled out into the road. "Go ahead," he answered a little more gruffly than he'd meant.

"I like it when you get all growly. Your voice is already deep, but when you get angry your voice gets even deeper. I mean like holy shit, it's panty melting." Her dancing brown eyes laughed at him.

"Sweetheart, I'll gladly melt your panties in any way you want me to." This game of tug of war, or one-upmanship, was surely gonna be the death of him. He shifted in the leather seat, trying to ease the tight constriction in his jeans. The way he was going, his poor abused dick would be the one with a permanent injury if he didn't get it out of his jeans. As soon as he got to his house, he was putting on a pair of loose sweats.

Chapter Three

Hailey licked her lips. "Promises, promises. I believe you're the one who's done nothing, but run in the opposite direction any time I've ever made anything resembling a pass at you."

Maddox scowled at her. "You're loco."

She watched him expertly maneuver them through traffic, then onto a side road she'd never been. "This isn't the way to the Steinem?"

He shook his head. "No. I'm taking us somewhere safe, and that is not it."

"I didn't know you had a place elsewhere." Although she should have. Heck, she herself had a home away from the apartment building. Why the others wouldn't, was the real question.

His truck bumped over a path that looked like it didn't get many visitors, making her worry her lower lip. She hadn't checked in with anyone letting them know where she was going, yet here she was going off with Maddox. Dex, a member of their team had tried to kill one of them not too long ago. Now, she was blindly assuming Maddox was one of the good guys. Fear tasted like ash on her tongue.

She grabbed her phone out of her bag. "I'm going to let JoJo know I'm with you. He doesn't know the location of this place, but if something should happen to me, then I want him to at least know who I was with." She hit the number for the other man on her speed dial.

When his voicemail picked up, she left a brief message and said she'd check back in every twelve hours. Maddox met her gaze across the console.

"Feel better, Hellion?"

"Not really. I hate not knowing who I can trust and who I can't." She put the phone back in her backpack.

He brought the truck to a stop, his large palm slid around the nape of her neck. "You know you can trust me." He tapped her chest with his finger of his other hand. "It's up here that has you all fucked up." His hand pushed the hair off her forehead, gently tapping her temple.

Sucking in much needed oxygen, she silently agreed. Her heart and her head warred with each other. No, she corrected. Her head also knew he was not the enemy.

She grabbed the hand lying on the console, loving the feel of the one caressing the nape of her neck. "I do trust you." Staring into his eyes, she let him see the truth of her words. Maddox wouldn't appreciate her giving him a line of bullshit, or painting him a flowery picture. Hell, she wasn't that type of woman.

He lifted their entwined hands, kissing her knuckles. "Good enough."

A laugh escaped her. "A man of few words."

"Hellion, you ain't heard or seen nothing yet."

Wicked intent lit his features, she couldn't wait to find out just what he had in store for her.

The home he pulled up to was a small log house that had been recently built if she wasn't mistaken. The A-frame structure common, with the front mostly windows that she could see all the way through to the back. "Nice place," she said.

Maddox smiled, getting out on his side and coming around to open her door. "Come on, let's go in and eat before our sandwiches go bad."

Handing the paper bag to him, she reached for her backpack, but pulled her hand back as Maddox lifted one of the straps over his shoulder. "I can carry my own stuff, you know."

"Keep getting lippy, and I'll toss you over my shoulder." He wagged his eyebrows, making her grin.

Inside the cabin he'd decorated with a leather and steel theme. "I like your place. Very masculine, yet minimalist."

He placed her backpack on top of the bar that acted as the kitchen table too. "It's not much, but it'll do. You want a drink?"

"Water please." Hailey hopped onto one of the swivel, high-top chairs. "How many bedrooms does this place have?"

It looked as if the bottom half was a totally open concept, but she could see stairs leading up to a loft.

His grin reminded her of the Cheshire Cat. She really did love that fluffy kitty. "There's one room up there with a big bed. Plenty of room for the both of us to stretch out without touching." He waited a beat. "Unless you want me to, and then I am all for touching you anywhere and everywhere."

With those words he picked up his deli sandwich and took a huge bite. Even white teeth smiled before he continued to eat, while she struggled to get oxygen into her starved brain. Her stomach reminded her she was hungry.

By the time he polished off his second sandwich, she finished her first and was ready for a shower. Rolling around in the dirt and gravel was only good if you were doing it for fun.

The sound of paper being scrunched up had her jerking back to see Maddox gathering up their trash. "Why don't you head on upstairs and take a shower. I need to set the alarm and check a few things."

A small reprieve from the man's presence, one she desperately needed or she'd make a total fool of herself. Nodding, she slid off the chair. "Thanks, Mad. I really am glad you were there today." She turned away before she broke down and said any more.

Taking the steps up to the loft, she glanced down to see him watching her. The open room had a view of trees that went on forever it seemed. But what caught her attention, was the king sized bed with the white comforter and the mound of pillows. "Damn, a person could get lost in all that fluffy goodness," she whispered as she walked by. Her body gravitated toward the bed, but she made herself continue to the open door where she could see a glass shower. Inside was what she'd expected. A shower big enough for two with smoked out blocks for privacy, a vanity and a toilet. Hanging on the towel rack, she saw he had two white towels, their softness was like hotel quality, and she wondered how the man paid for such luxury for a secondary home. It made her realize she didn't know all that much about him.

"Shit, I need conditioner." Shrugging, knowing nothing she did would change the fact she didn't have the basic necessities.

In her backpack she always kept an extra change of clothes, and some makeup. She'd kill for a toothbrush, and moisturizer.

Not wanting to dawdle, she shimmied out of her clothes, tossing them off to the side, then stepped inside the shower, happy to see Maddox actually had a good quality shampoo and conditioner. The man shaved his head, which raised the question of who was the owner of the product. Hailey wasn't one to get jealous, but admitted the little monster tried to rear its head, then she reminded herself to be glad since she had something to use. "It's none of my business if he has a new hussy each day of the week," she mumbled to herself.

Maddox parked his truck in the garage attached to the side of the cabin, then made sure the security was set to high. He looked at the cameras that were all around the property, making sure the motion sensors were working. With the door shut to the one room that was separate from the rest on the main floor, he called Mike.

"What up, bro?"

"My blood pressure," Maddox flipped the screen to the camera in the upstairs bedroom, catching a glimpse of Hailey running her fingers over the bed.

Mike chuckled. "I just bet it is. Wanna swap places? I'll gladly take over guard duty for that piece of ass."

It took monumental effort not to say what he wanted. Instead, he grit his teeth. "You got anything useful for me, or just wanting to yank my chain?"

A heavy sigh came through the line. "The men who were following you, were no amateurs. Lucky for you, I'm better, and have a better set of skills than they possess. Not to mention a lot more toys."

He knew Mike wasn't just bragging. The man was lethal personified. Hell, if you needed a person killed, Royce was the one to call. No matter the way you needed the job done. Thankfully, he was on the good guy's team. "Please tell me the bodies aren't going to be on my account?" Each time they had to bury a body, Uncle Sam tended to get a little pissy. Of course, he'd get a whole lot more so if they didn't take care of the terrorists in question.

"Pretty sure I made certain they had my tags on them."

Even through the phone, Maddox heard the shrug in Mike's tone. The camera to the room showed Hailey going into the bathroom. His dick twitched as the door stayed open, images of her wet and naked nearly sent him running out of the room, and up to where she was. Only years of training, and self-control kept him from acting on the urges running through his mind.

"Keep me posted if you hear anything, and I'll do the same. You got eyes on me here?"

"Does a bear shit in the woods? Get the fuck outta here, man. What do you think? Never mind, don't answer that, or I'll have to kick your ass. I gotta go. My show is on," Mike said.

"Which one are you addicted to now? Real Housewives of the OC or New York?" Maddox watched the night vision cameras flip on, alerting him to the fact the sun had set.

"Laugh all you want, but I am learning lots of useful shit from these women. And, for your information, it's New Jersey." Mike disconnected before Maddox could say anymore.

Shaking his head, Maddox pictured his partner kicked back watching the reality show. While Maddox was what some might consider tall, dark and dangerous, Mike Royce was almost pretty boy gorgeous. His dark hair was shoulder length, but the man always had it pulled back. His dark complexion and tall build made him stand out in a crowd, but it was his emerald green eyes that had people taking a second look. When he sat a person down, and *talked* to them, they tended to spill their guts. Of course, his two hundred and fifty pounds of muscle, and no nonsense attitude, didn't hurt either.

"Fucking better not have pinned any of your shit on me, Royce," he muttered switching the cameras to high alert. He synced them to his watch in case an alarm was set off, knowing his partner would be alerted as well.

The walk up to the loft took very little time, but he didn't want to scare Hailey. "Yo, Hales. I'm just going to grab a few things, then I'll bunk on the sofa downstairs."

He'd been too preoccupied on his trek up the stairs, he hadn't noticed the shower was no longer running. His mouth watered as Hailey appeared in the doorway wearing nothing but one of the fluffy towels from the bathroom. In that moment, he wished they were a lot smaller, yet thanked the lord they were covering her at the same time. Yeah, he was a little skewed in his thinking, and it was the fault of the little hellion standing in front of him with the smirk on her face.

"What's the matter, Mad, something wrong?" She trailed the toes of one foot up her leg, bringing his attention to her dainty foot.

"You paint your toenails polka dot?" he asked. The whimsical art seemed out of character for the woman he knew.

"I switch it up." Her shoulders lifted and fell, making the towel move with the action.

He licked his lips. "I'll give you one of my shirts to sleep in, if you'd like."

The little minx sauntered out of the bathroom. "That would be great. I have clean panties, but only a pair of yoga pants and a tank for tomorrow. I really didn't want to sleep in them."

"Alright. Let me get it for you, then I'll let you have the room." Her hand on his arm stopped him.

"Mad, I think we are both old enough, and mature enough we don't need to sleep in separate spaces." She smiled up at him.

His mind agreed, but his body wasn't on the same level. "Sure. I'll just get you the shirt, and then shower. I feel like I got gravel between my teeth." Maddox grabbed a black T-shirt for Hailey and a clean pair of boxer briefs for himself out of the drawer.

"Pretty sure I washed away a butt load of dirt and gravel myself. Not to mention, there are probably some pretty colorful bruises appearing all over my ass." Her playful tone had him laughing.

"And on that note, I'll be in taking a cold shower."

Unlike Hailey, he shut the bathroom door, needing that little barrier between himself and the woman who was slowly driving him crazy. Or crazier, depending on who you asked. He thought of easing the ache between his legs, but decided against it. Hell, his right hand had become Hailey number two in the last year or so. No need to announce it to the woman on the other side of the door. Noticing the shampoo and conditioner on the ledge, he groaned. Fucking Royce and his hair care products. Hailey probably thought it was his lover's or some shit.

He quickly washed his body, feeling small aches from his own roll over the hard unforgiving ground. Outside the shower he grabbed the last towel on the rack and dried off, then scooped their dirty laundry up. He'd throw them into the wash later. At the mirror his shaving cream was tucked inside the cabinet, reminding him the stubble on top his head needed shaving. Grabbing the razor and a wash cloth, he lathered up, making quick work of shaving his head and face. Once he was done, he ran his palm over both.

Enough time had passed, he hoped like hell she was in bed. If the lord was smiling on him, maybe she'd be fast asleep. He shut the light off before opening the bathroom door, breathing a sigh of relief when he saw she'd taken up a position on one side of the bed. His muscles froze as his eyes adjusted to the darkened room, taking in the view of Hailey, lying on her side facing away from him. The blanket had fallen away, giving him a perfect view of her gorgeous heart shaped ass. "I'm going to fucking hell," he muttered, looking down at his erection. The boxer briefs couldn't disguise his state if he'd tried. His only saving grace was the fact she'd clearly fallen asleep and faced away from him. A quick glance at his watch showed it was just after ten, but they'd had an eventful day. Double checking the parameters of the property on his smart watch showed nothing had set off the alarms, other than the animals.

Thinking he should have put something else on to sleep in other than just his boxers for added barriers, but even a brick wall wouldn't keep his dick from wanting the woman. He shrugged and sat on the opposite side of the bed. The thought he'd sleep on top of the covers flittered through his mind, then was dismissed. They were grown adults like she'd said. Mind made up, he stood, pulled the blanket back, and got in next to Hailey. Clearly, she'd chucked half the mound of pillows onto the floor. He held back a laugh, wishing he'd been there to have seen how she'd selected which to keep, and which to toss off.

In the dark, he folded his arms behind his head, and thought about the attempt on her life. The shooters had missed, yet she was a large target. In his mind, that meant they were either really bad shots, or they hadn't meant to kill her. Her bike being blown to bits with her not on it was another conundrum in his mind. Of course, a professional wouldn't have rigged it to go off at a certain time, not wanting to gamble with the fact she may or may not be on it. However, a professional clearly had been watching, and set the bomb off without her on it, or it was a screwed up time.

Either option didn't sit well with him as that meant someone still wanted Hailey dead.

He let out a big sigh.

"Stop thinking. Especially if it hurts too much." Hailey's drowsy voice broke through his musings.

"I'd swat your ass, but I'm not sure where your colorful bruises are. I thought you were sleeping," he said keeping his voice low.

The sound of the covers rustling announced her rolling over to face him. "I was trying. But then I got to thinking about the attempts on my life today."

His mind froze as she echoed what he'd been thinking. "So you think there were two different factions, not one trying twice?" he asked to be clear.

She propped her head on her left arm. "That's what I'm thinking. How about you?"

He rolled over and mimicked her pose. "Yeah. I also don't think these were professional hits."

"No shit. Hell, most amateurs could have at least hit me once. It's not like I was under the cover of trees or anything. A big open space with nothing to impede their shot, except you. Pretty sure that wasn't what stopped them from hitting vital parts." Her snort was too cute for words.

Maddox pulled himself up short at his thoughts. He didn't think women's snorts were cute for fucking crying out loud. Nor their polka dot toenails. "I'll make a few inquiries tomorrow. Until then, don't reach out to anyone. This doesn't smell right to me."

He'd been in the CIA long enough to know when there was more going on behind the scenes than a simple operation. Hell, he was on an operation under the guise of being a SEAL for the Navy. Not that he hadn't completed all the skills needed, and then some to be a SEAL. He'd been cherry picked from the batch when his test scores reflected a higher level of aptitude. Thankfully his best friend since childhood had been too, otherwise Maddox didn't think he'd have signed on. Or at least he liked to pretend they had a choice. They'd seen enough in the seventeen years since graduating from high school and enlisting.

"How about you? Can I reach out to you?" Her breath hitched.

"Sweetheart, you can reach out to me anytime, anywhere you want. Just know I will be more than you are probably ready for. Consider that before you think about playing cat and mouse. I'm not the type of man who lets little girls tease, or one who is a pussy by any stretch of the imagination. The only thing a pussy and me have in common is the fact I enjoy them. I love the way they look, the way they taste, or when I fuck them with my fingers. I especially love the way they feel wrapped around my cock, watching them stretch to take me inside," he growled.

Chapter Four

Maddox had no clue why he was saying what he was, other than it was the truth. Yes, he was a dominant with his lovers, but he'd never thought to lay it out like he was with Hailey. Any second, and he was sure she'd toss the cover off and storm out.

"Holy shit, I think I may be the one who needs to take a cold shower."

To say he was beyond stunned would be an understatement. "We need to get some rest, Hales."

If she thought she needed a cold shower, he needed a freaking ice cold one. He regretted not rubbing one out earlier.

"You do realize I am not a virgin, right? I mean, I'm a healthy twenty-nine year old woman. I've had a few lovers over the years. Albeit, not as many as I'm sure you've had, but still, I am not some shy and retiring..."

Maddox rolled over, covering her mouth with his. Hearing her talk of past lovers, his and hers wasn't something he wanted to think about. The soft exclamation she made was swallowed by him. As he licked inside her mouth, she dueled with his tongue for supremacy, making him laugh inside. Careful of her injuries, he reached for her hands, holding them in one of his above her head. He pulled back, nibbled on her lower lip, then the top only to return to the bottom and suck it into his mouth. This close he could see her eyes widen as he loomed over her.

"For the record, I'm glad you're not a virgin. I haven't deflowered one of them in over ten years. I much prefer feisty blondes with big brown eyes." He wedged his left leg between her thighs, the feel of her silken panties thrilled him. "Are you wet, Hellion?"

She pulled her lower lip into her mouth. "Only one way to find out, big guy. I do believe you said something about being BFF with pussies. Mine is friendless at the moment."

"Damn, you are the only woman who can turn my words around on me." He let his leg move up, giving her a little of what he knew she needed.

Hailey moaned. "Your words are a form of foreplay, I swear."

He froze, the fact he'd used his charms in the past made him hesitate. Hailey wasn't a mark. He wasn't doing anything, for any reason, other than the man in him wanted to.

"Hey, where did you go?" she asked, her arms jerking against his grip.

"Nowhere, sorry." Looking down into her face, the moon casting shadows across them, Maddox thought she was the most beautiful woman he'd ever seen.

Uncertainty blinked up at him. "Do you have a girlfriend or...?"

Hating that he'd caused her to question his sincerity, he released her hands, coming down onto his elbows on each side of her head. "First of all, I think you know me a little better than that, Hales. Second, I have wanted you since the first time I walked into the Steinem Building and saw you standing in a pair of green cargo pants and a yellow tank top. You had your hair pulled up in a ponytail, your sunglasses were resting on the top of your head, and your backpack was slung over one shoulder. I had to stop and count to a hundred before I could approach the counter, just to get my dick to deflate, otherwise JoJo would have been hard pressed not to recognize the erection I was sporting. Now, you tell me I am not interested, or haven't been interested in you. Hell, my right hand thinks its name is Hailey for crying out loud."

With each word, her body lost some of its rigidity, until she was smiling beneath him. "So, no Rosie for you?"

Chuckling, he rubbed his nose against her neck. "Is that all you got from my declaration?"

"I can tell you down to what color your socks were, what you were wearing the first time I saw you. And my BOB is named Mad, so we are even. And, I think my local grocer thinks I'm doing something crazy with all the double D batteries I go through." She squirmed beneath him.

"Damn! If I'd have known that, I would have swung by your place to pick him up," he joked.

Hailey tried to pinch his side. "Alright, so since we've each shared some intimate details, and neither of us are virgins. What's next?"

Maddox rested his forehead against hers. "I should probably let you sleep. You've been shot at, your bike blown up, and you have a slight concussion. I have to wake you every couple of hours, remember?"

"Or, we could go with plan B."

He looked down and waited to hear what she was thinking. The feel of her cool, slim fingers sliding into his boxer briefs had him groaning. "That's your plan B?"

Fingers wrapping around his cock was his answer.

"I swear to all that is holy, you are going to be the death of me." He shuddered. "Fuck that feels good."

"Better than Rosie?"

Nodding he lifted away to give her better access. "Oh yeah. Rosie has calluses."

She squeezed a little harder.

Tired of not touching, he hadn't been lying when he said he loved all things pussy, he adjusted his weight to one side, and trailed his left hand down her side. "I think we need to take this off. It offends me."

She laughed. "Why is that?"

He helped her take his T-shirt off. "Cause its covering these glorious breasts. Yes. I knew they were perfect." He bent and took one hardened tip into his mouth.

"Too small," she gasped.

He gave a small bite, letting her know he didn't agree. The slight sting had her tensing, then she sighed. "You like that?" he asked.

"A little too much, I'm afraid. Will you do it again, just to make sure?"

His little hellion. Gladly, he treated the other nipple to the same treatment, trailing his fingers into her panties. Wetness greeted him, and as he bit down, more of her juices flowed, wetting his fingers. He looked down, wishing he'd had a light on to see if her body flushed when she was aroused, and promised he'd leave a light on next time.

"You're so damn wet. I'm gonna have to taste. See if you're as sweet as I'd fantasized about."

"I want to taste you, too. I couldn't even get my fingers around Little Mad."

Nearly choking on his words, he ran his fingers through her silken folds. "I'm going to ignore your name for my junk." His mouth watered for a taste of her, he licked his fingers clean. "Come here." He moved to the middle of the bed and laid flat, pulling his briefs off while she sat up. "Hales, you change your mind?"

"God, no." She wasted no time taking her panties off. Then, as he ran his hand up and down his shaft, she crawled the few feet over to him.

Maddox reached up with his right hand, palming the nape of her neck he brought her head down to his. Her hand joined his left one, pumping his dick in slow easy thrusts. Finally, when he was sure she was no longer scared, he pulled her back from the kiss.

Hailey bent over his body and took his dick into her mouth. Maddox struggled to remember he wanted to taste her. Grabbing her by the hips, he easily lifted her until she was straddling his face. She squeaked, her hands going onto his thighs to steady herself.

"It's alright, Hales. I got you. Damn, I bet you're even pretty here." He ran his palms over her ass, then held her open with his thumbs, and started to pleasure Hailey. So fucking good.

Her legs and hips began a slow gyrate as she chased her own pleasure. Maddox found her clit, and with fast hard licks had her close to coming.

"Maddox. More. I need..." Her hand froze on his dick.

He grabbed the bundle of nerves between his teeth, lashing it with his tongue, then pushed two fingers into her. Her scream was music to his ears.

Licking her through her orgasm, he continued to move his fingers in a slow pulse, knowing it would heighten her pleasure.

"God, you are a fucking rock star at that. I don't think I have ever come so quick or hard in my entire life." She panted, and crawled away from him.

"Hey, you're taking my treat."

She sat up on her knees, pulling her hair back from her face and tying it back with a band from her wrist. "Now, since you distracted me too much for me to give LM the proper attention, let me make amends."

Maddox laughed. He'd never laughed so much in bed with a woman before. "Please, go forth and do what you feel is best." He waved at his dick lying on his stomach. The thing was too hard and heavy to do anything else.

"Poor guy. He's so dejected." Hailey got between his knees, scraping her blunt nails down his thighs. It took all his control not to grab her by the back of the head, and demand she suck him.

Instead, he balled his hands into fists at his sides. He'd give her a few minutes to play, then he'd take over. It was in his nature, he made no apologies. Although, he did make sure his women were well fucked, and left with no hard feelings.

She licked around the crown of his cock, then down the heavy vein, tickling the sensitive underside. Sheot! His balls drew up by the fourth pass like an untried youth. She'd called him a rock star, but she was the one schooling him with a mouth that was made for sucking.

Unable to keep from grabbing her, his hand reached for the ponytail at the back of her head. Guiding her in the rhythm he needed. She bobbed up and down on him, licking and sucking while moving her hand up and down. He placed his own fist on the base of his shaft to keep from forcing her to take too much.

"That's it. Fuckin-A, Hales," he groaned. "Ease up. I'm going to come."

His words had her holding him tighter, her mouth covered the crown, and then she took him as far back as she could, swallowing around the head. He was sure he saw stars, maybe even Jesus as his orgasm started in his toes and worked its way through his entire body like a tsunami. Jet after jet of come, and still his hellion continued to swallow and work him over till he had nothing else to give. Long seconds after he was sure he'd passed out, he felt her tongue on him, licking him clean.

"Hales, if I was a rock star at eating pussy, you are a rock goddess at giving head." He brushed his knuckles down her cheek.

She placed a kiss on his spent dick. "Hot damn. We could start our own band." She yawned.

"Come here." He reached down and pulled her up to lie beside him. "Get some rest. I'll wake you in a couple hours."

With his left arm, he pulled the comforter over them.

"You're bossy," she paused. "I like that about you."

"I hope you remember that in a couple hours and don't bite my head off." He wrapped his arms around a woman for the first time in bed before falling asleep.

Hailey groaned as Maddox tried waking her for the third time. "Mad, seriously. I think we can safely rule I'm fine." She burrowed under the pillow.

His chuckle had her reaching for his side to pinch. "Hey, that's not nice, Hales. Want me to pinch you?"

She rubbed against the growing erection with her ass. "Hmm, I think that thing wants to do something other than pinch me."

"Ignore him. He always wakes up that way." A slight adjustment and Maddox was gliding between her thighs from behind.

"Newsflash! It's hard to ignore something that is rubbing you in all the right spots," she said breathlessly.

"Want me to stop?" he asked, pulling back.

Looking over her shoulder, she met his green gaze. "Got a condom?"

"Does a bear shit in the woods?" He used the same phrase his friend Mike used the day before.

"Unless they live in a zoo, yes." She lifted her leg, giving him more room to move back and forth.

The swat to her ass surprised her, the heat lit up nerve endings that had an answering zing throughout her entire body. "You are a brat." He rolled away from her.

Thinking she'd pushed him too far, she turned to watch him open the drawer on the nightstand. He ripped the foil packet with his teeth, then met her gaze. "Put it on for me. Be good, or I'll teach you some manners." Anticipation marked his gaze.

She plucked the condom from between his two fingers. Once she made sure which side was the proper way to roll it on, she smoothed it down, marveling at his size. "Yes, Sir. I promise to be a good girl from here on out."

"Little liar." He gave her a heated look that let her know he looked forward to her brattiness. Hailey had never found a man she could be herself with in bed. One she could let take charge, and loved how easy it was to allow Maddox complete control.

The push he gave her was another gentle reminder that he was in charge, and she went willingly. When he climbed over her this time, she immediately gave him her hands.

"Keep them above your head, Hellion." His voice had gone deeper.

Moving her legs on the outside of his, she licked her lips. "Yes, Sir."

Maddox smiled. "Good girl."

When he bent, his lips brushed hers, teasing, tempting. Hailey followed where he led. His big body dwarfing hers. He settled on his knees and looked down at her, giving her a wink. She knew he was dominating, but when he ran his hands from the top of her shoulders, down to her ankles, moving her thighs farther apart, she tensed, waiting to see what he'd do next, wondering what his next assault on her senses would be. Maddox was not a man to disappoint, trailing kisses from her throat down to her breasts, making her arch in anticipation.

She gasped as he took the tip of one nipple into his mouth, and inserted a finger into her at the same time. The dual assault had her shaking. He brushed feather-light kisses down her stomach, and then his mouth was covering her pussy. The exquisite feelings were exactly what she'd come to expect, yet she wanted to be filled by more.

"You taste delicious in the morning, Hales." Maddox's deep voice added another layer of sensation to her exposed flesh. His fingers teased her clit, sliding through her labia, parting her folds as he slowly glided his tongue up and down, lighting nerve endings. "Maddox please," she begged. It felt amazing, but still not enough. Not what she needed.

He licked her in forceful strokes, taking her to a fast orgasm. His finger reached up and plucked at her nipple, rolling it between thumb and forefinger.

"Tell me what you want, Hellion," he demanded. Maddox lifted his head, her arousal coating his chin and lips.

"I want you to fuck me, Mad," she answered breathlessly.

He moaned, pushing in two fingers and curling them. Hailey's fingers clawed at the bedding, her hips moved up and down, fucking herself on his pumping fingers.

"You're so damn tight I fear I'll blow as soon as I stick my dick in you." Maddox watched her with his gorgeous green eyes hooded with lust.

She whimpered. "I'm right there, Mad. I want to come with you in me."

Her words must have been what he was waiting for. He moved up her body, guiding himself into her with a gentleness that amazed and endeared Hailey.

"Fuck me running. Tight, so good. I knew you would be," he gritted out. Maddox eased down onto his elbows as he worked his way in slowly, the effort showing on his face.

Hailey sucked in a breath at the fullness. Inch by inch, he gained ground, nibbling on her ear, whispering how good she felt, and for the first time she felt loved. She quickly shut down that train of thought and concentrated on the here and now. She shivered as he slid out, then pushed back in, his pace picking up.

"Damn, Hales, you are even tighter than I imagined. You sure you're not a virgin?" He held himself still above her.

She responded by locking her legs around his waist and lifting her hips to take him deeper. "You are just incredibly well-endowed, and my last lover was over two years ago, if you don't count BOB."

He stopped moving. "Next time I'll be sure and grab him too, just so we can compare." The growled words held an edge of danger.

A laugh bubbled out of her. "I'm not sure about that. Clearly, I should have bought the larger size. Now, could you move...Sir?" She squeezed her inner muscles, knowing he'd feel them and hopefully be inclined to move.

He started to shake, then laughed out loud. "Damn woman, you surprise me at every turn." He leaned down and kissed her, his tongue pushed past her lips, fucking her mouth the same as he was her body. He cursed, pushing up onto his hands and stared down at her. "Hard and fast, baby. You ready to come?"

She could only nod. Watching his face bunch up and the muscles in his arms and shoulders flex were a sight to behold.

On each downward thrust, he swiveled his hips against her clit, making her moan. Every muscle in her body tensed, starting in her toes, and ending in her pussy, rolling over her like a tidal wave. She cried out as tremors shook her. Maddox continued to thrust in and out, prolonging her pleasure. She heard him shout as he came, thrusting one last time, then holding himself against her. She didn't care that her arms were supposed to stay above her head, she needed to hold him. Running her hands over his smooth back, she knew one time, a stolen moment with her rogue SEAL wouldn't be enough.

Chapter Five

Hailey closed her eyes as she felt Maddox pull away. She searched her mind for words to say, but nothing came to her. The man was an enigma. He was her partner, sort of.

"I'll be right back." Maddox gave her a crooked grin, then climbed off the bed. She watched his muscled ass flex as he went into the bathroom.

The sound of the shower running had her looking up at the ceiling with a sigh. "Get up and start breakfast Hales. Don't lay around waiting for him to come back and show you some attention." She slid off the side of the bed, searching for the T-shirt from the night before, and headed down the steps toward the kitchen. She made a quick stop in the bathroom downstairs first, then went to see what he had to make for breakfast. Her first stop was the coffee pot. God, she really needed some of the liquid gold.

Once she got the fancy machine started, she opened the fridge. "Bacon and eggs it is." Whenever she was nervous, she tended to talk to herself, a habit she hated, but couldn't seem to stop.

After the first cup, she felt almost normal. The scent of bacon frying along with the eggs perfumed the air, and still no sign of Maddox. Covering the bacon with some foil, she turned the oven on warm, and set the eggs inside.

The subtle sound of glass smashing had her hurrying toward the stairs. It was a sound she would know anywhere. She wished like hell she'd thought to grab her backpack, but had not thought for one moment that she'd need it. Her heart raced as she eased up the stairs. The third step squeaked she'd noted earlier and this time she made sure to skip it all together. No sound, save for her own heartbeat, and the slight puffs of air broke through the quietness. As she reached the top of the landing, she crouched down to make her way into the bedroom.

Steam from the shower still hung in the air. With no visible sign of Maddox, she tiptoed to where she'd left her bag. Her mind raced, thinking of the exits and what was going on. If someone had broken in, where were they?

Shaking her head, she palmed her gun after making sure it was loaded. Her extra pair of pants were quickly pulled out and on, then she was moving toward the bathroom. Back against the wall, a sick feeling welled up. An image of what she might find inside the small room popped into her mind. She breathed deeply. Her hands were steady as they held her Sig Sauer. The weight of the weapon giving her comfort as she moved into the room. Water still dripped from the shower, but she could see the window had been knocked out. A towel lay over it like someone had done it on purpose.

Hailey stilled and went to the shower, pulling back the curtain to find it empty. She breathed a ragged sigh. Where the fuck was Maddox? With the glass inside, she deduced blunt force from outside had broken it.

The loud crack of gun fire broke through the quietness, echoing through her veins. Making her way over to the window she paid closer attention to the towel, and the smear of bright red blood. She could barely see down to the ground from the upper level, but the balcony outside the bathroom window ran all the way around the back of the A-frame structure. The size of the hole was large enough for a man, but if Maddox had gone out willingly, why hadn't he alerted her?

A quick glance around, and the thought that she was a sitting duck hit her. She moved back to the bedroom, shoved her feet into her shoes and pulled a hoodie out of her bag. Her cellphone needed charging, but she was able to shoot a text to JoJo, letting him know in a few words what had happened.

"What the heck? Where are you?" JoJo's text came back.

Hailey didn't have time to explain, only wanted them to know who she was with and what had happened. "I'm turning on my app that will allow you to locate me just in case something happens. Don't do anything stupid."

"I'm calling in reinforcements which you should've done when you were nearly killed." The quick response made tears come to her eyes. The guys had become like a second family to her. JoJo and Blake were like brothers from another mother.

She turned the sound off of her phone and shoved it into the pocket of the hoodie, sending up a silent prayer to anyone who would listen to keep them all safe. Dammit, where was Mad?

A creak had her eyes flaring. She knew exactly what that sound was and where it came from. Her training kicked in, making her eternally grateful she was able to push back the fear. Her nerves were steady as she went to stand by the wall, and waited for whomever to come through the door. Even as her pulse raced, scenarios ran through her mind. A glance at the mirror showed the stark white face staring back at herself. Time ticked by at a slow pace, but she held her position, not daring to breathe loudly. Her hand tightened slightly on the trigger. Fucking hell, she hated this. Her body tensed as the air thickened with expectation.

Maddox moved up the stairway. He'd chased after the shooter when the bullet had whizzed past his head. Foolishly, he'd thought for sure he could catch him before he'd disappeared. Why the hell hadn't any of the security alarms alerted them to an intruder?

His gut twisted as he reached the top, and heard no movement. He hadn't even thought twice about leaving Hailey alone in the cabin, unprotected, and vulnerable. Foolishly, he'd assumed the shooter was the only one out there. Now, he made his way up to the bedroom after searching the lower half with his heart in his throat.

Taking a deep breath, his Glock in his fist, he eased around the doorframe, then pulled up short. Faced with a petite woman holding a gun at his head, he didn't think he'd ever find himself happier in his entire life. Breath whooshed out of him. "You scared the shit out of me, Hales."

The gun didn't lower or waiver. "Where have you been?"

He narrowed his eyes. "Put the gun down."

She shook her head. "What the hell has happened here, Mad? I hear glass breaking, then come up here to find you gone, and then this." She waved at him, her tone flat.

Oh hell. Maddox moved forward, eliminating the space between them. "I'd just gotten dressed and finished shaving, when I dropped my towel. I bent to pick it up. I'm pretty sure that is the only thing that saved my life. Once I realized there was a shooter, I took the towel and put it over the window, and saw him on the balcony. Fucker was that close, and I didn't even sense him." He was still disgusted by that fact.

Her sigh mirrored his. "Why did you chase him without letting me know?"

"You gonna shoot me or lower that damn gun?" He growled, tired of getting shot at.

"Did you get a look at him or her?" She placed her weapon in the back of her pants.

Maddox swore it was the sexiest thing he'd seen in a long time. "Not really. He was dressed in black and didn't look to be much bigger than me, only slimmer. Hell, I'm trying to figure out why the security alarms didn't go off."

Hailey worried her bottom lip. The last thing he wanted to do was go back to work, when he could think of other things she could do with that perfect bow shaped mouth. He lifted his free hand and tugged her lip free from her teeth. "Come on, we need to get out of here, this location has been compromised." His side ached from the wound.

"You've been shot," she whispered moving forward to touch him.

Her concern caused the part of his anatomy, he was sure only worked to keep him alive, to beat double time. Hell, Royce would laugh his ass off if he could hear his internal dialogue. His breath sucked in as her slim fingers lifted his blood soaked shirt. "It's only a graze, I've had worse."

Milk chocolate eyes narrowed up at him. "I've heard that one before, big guy."

He gripped her wrist in his fingers. "Baby, we need to go. Once we get to where we're going, I'll let you play nurse. But this guy, however amateur he was may not have been alone."

A nod was his answer, but he felt the shiver she couldn't hide. Damn, he fucking hated seeing her fear. This place should have been a safe haven, one so far off the radar nobody should've known about it. He wondered how anyone could have found them. Eyes narrowed, he glanced down at the little spitfire.

"What is that look, Mad?"

"Give me your phone." When she didn't immediately comply, a tic began in the corner of his eye.

"Don't be crazy. I hadn't even called or texted anyone until I found you missing."

The roaring in his ears nearly sent him to his knees. "Hales, the phone," he demanded.

"Fine, but what if something happens to me?"

He shrugged. "You've got me watching your back. I'd say you're in good hands."

His little hellion actually blushed, something he was sure she would never do. As she handed him the phone, he let his fingers brush over hers, tracing the faint blue veins. With efficiency he looked through her apps, seeing the fact she'd activated the find me app recently. He gave her a sidelong look, sighing at her naiveté. He didn't have time to check her phone for bugs, or tracking devices, and knew what he was about to do was likely to get her all riled up. Mad, was looking forward to making her pay for what she does and says next. With precision, he set the phone back to factory settings, then dropped it before stomping it to bits.

"Damn it, Mad, that was the latest iPhone. Do you know how much that thing is going to cost to replace?" She knelt down by the bits of metal and glass.

"We don't have time to fuck around, Hales. Get up." He smoothed his hand over her hair, instead of grabbing it in his fist.

"Fine, but you are buying me a new goddamn phone, Maddox Lopez. A rose fucking pink one, too." She stood up, poking him in the chest with each word.

Her words had his dick hard, and his inner dom standing at attention. "How do you end that sentence, Hellion?"

She licked her lips. "Sir?"

Knowing time was ticking, but wanting to solidify his control, he bent the few inches, placing his lips next to her ear. "Good girl. Let's go."

As she went to grab her backpack, he shook his head. "Leave it. If someone knows you, then they know you always take that thing. There could be a tracking device anywhere on it, or in it."

"What about that monster truck you have?"

Ignoring her outburst, he snagged her hand and pulled her behind him. Precious little darling had no idea the swats she was earning with her back talking. He shook his head but ignored her struggles. On the bottom level, they went toward the security room. His palm print opened the door.

"The oven is on. I cooked for us." She blushed, then shook her head. "How the hell did I not see this?"

"I already took care of the food. As for this." He inclined his head. "You weren't supposed to." The wall slid open, revealing the secret room. Once inside, he made sure the door closed securely behind them. "Come on." Another door hidden behind a large map revealed the thick steel escape door to the outside. Automatic lights came on as they entered and descended the steps down. "Watch your step. This escape was designed for efficiency, not comfort."

At the bottom, he waited, looking around for signs that anyone had trespassed. The dust hadn't been disturbed, a clear sign nobody had been there since the last time he'd visited. They made their way back up, her steps as sure as his, barely making a sound. Maddox couldn't fault her abilities as a soldier. Twenty minutes later, he was sure his side had stopped bleeding just as they came to the end. He held up his hand, indicating they needed to stop.

Hailey quirked a brow, watching him open up the live feed.

"All clear." He used his palm again to open the locking mechanism.

"Damn, fancy machinery you gots here, Sir."

Maddox swatted her on the ass. "Don't get sassy with me."

She touched his side. "You got a med kit around here? If we don't treat this, this might get infected."

Her concern touched him. "I'll let you tend to me when we are far away from here." The door took some effort to get open, filtered light spilled in.

"Where the hell are we?" Hailey's hand touched his back.

"A good distance from the property." He didn't want to say too much as he still wasn't sure, how much trust to put into the woman who held too much power over him. "Let's go. We should be clear. Once we get in the car, I'm going to have you lie in the back and stay low. If they are on the road searching, they'll be looking for a couple."

Moving quickly, he led the way to the bunker hidden into the side of the hill. Once he used his access code to open the door, they entered to find an older model SUV that looked like a beater. Maddox knew for a fact looks were deceiving. Not wanting to dwell on thoughts of duplicity, he grabbed the extra gear bag, and checked it was complete with what he'd need. A ball cap covered his head, giving him a slight change in appearance.

"You don't fully trust me," she said without heat.

He sighed. "It's not that I don't trust you, but someone had to have tracked us to the cabin. I know I didn't call anyone. That leaves only one other person, Hales. So, it's not that I don't trust you, but I am trying to save our asses, while my ass is dealing with a bullet wound."

"Well, fuck you very much, asshole. I was shot at yesterday, and my bike was blown to kingdom come. The last damn thing I would want to do is wave a goddamn flag at the ones who tried to kill me, by letting them know where I was fucking the morning away." Hailey turned away, but he saw the tears in her eyes.

Maddox felt like the asshole she'd called him. "Come here, Hailey." He put his hand on her shoulder.

"Don't. Just don't. I would stomp out of here, if I knew where here was. However, one thing I'm not is an idiot." She opened the back passenger door and got inside, shutting him out.

"Well, I for one, am not a happy camper you shut me out of what was clearly a good morning," Royce muttered through the earpiece.

"Fucking dickhead," Maddox growled too low for Hailey to hear.

The chuckle in his ear set his teeth on edge.

When he got into the Bronco, Hailey was sitting in the middle of the bench seat. He noticed she'd buckled up, and with a nod he started the engine then backed out. Jumping out once they were clear, he made sure the door was shut and hidden again. The entire fiasco took less than ten minutes, but he could feel her angry stare burning holes into him.

He couldn't leave things as they were. "Hales, I'm sorry. Truly, I'm a dick and I shouldn't have accused you of the bullshit that went down. I know you had nothing to do with what happened back at the cabin."

She gave a short jerky nod. "Thanks. What are your plans?"

"That's it? Fuck me. I said I was sorry." For him that was huge.

Growing up with a family who had always thought she was a screw up, she had promised she'd never be in the same position again. Especially not with a man she cared about. Flowery words were not going to make it okay for him to treat her like shit.

His arm flexed across the space between the driver seat and passenger, but he didn't reach back to shake some sense into her. Points for him.

"Hailey, think about it. You called JoJo. Now, I am not saying he betrayed us. Just consider the fact your phone may have been bugged, or had a trace put on it long before we arrived here. Hell, maybe it was my phone. Although, I haven't made a call since before I tracked you down on the side of the road."

She listened to his explanations, and realized she was being a bit of a bitch. Of course, he had accused her first. She rubbed at her temples. "Fine, let's call a truce."

"Can I have a kiss?" He pushed out his lower lip.

Never would she have thought in a hundred years to see the big bad Maddox pretending to be a baby. Well, she amended, a sexy man with a sexy lower lip needing to be sucked. Almost babyish in her mind. Unsnapping her seatbelt, she closed the distance between their mouths and kissed him. The awkward position made it difficult, and she wished they were anywhere except on the run so they could do more.

He grimaced. "I'd give my left nut to toss your ass in that backseat and fuck you good and proper."

"Pretty sure fucking in the backseat, and good and proper, have nothing in common," she snorted.

A laugh boomed out of Maddox. "Point taken. Buckle up, baby. We may be in for a rough ride. Remember my rule about ducking down. I want you to stay low, and if I say hit the floor, I mean hit the floor," he growled, then pulled her to him for another scorching kiss.

"Yes, Sir," she panted.

Her hands felt much clumsier buckling up the second time than they did the first. She met his heated gaze in the rearview mirror, promise in his dark gaze. To say the man had panty-melting looks was a major understatement.

He bumped along a track only he seemed to know, while she did all she could to not slam into the roof or doors depending on which way they turned. By the time they hit the road, she was sure she'd cracked a tooth from clenching her teeth and worried her ass may be fractured.

"I'll kiss your ass when we get where we're going," Maddox said with a grin over his shoulder, making her realize she'd said the last out loud.

She raised her right hand, middle finger extended, giving him the bird.

"Ah, Hales, you don't even know the enjoyment I'm going to get when I make you pay for that little infraction." Maddox kept his eyes on the road, but the threat was clear.

She wasn't sure why she kept pushing his buttons, but the idea of Maddox turning her over his lap had everything feminine in her squirming with gleeful anticipation.

"Oh yeah. I know that expression. I bet you anything if I was to put my hand down your panties, you'd be dripping that sweet cream for me." Maddox's tongue came out and licked his lips.

Her breath shuddered out at his words. "You'd be right. I think for you, I might be in a perpetual state of horniness."

He grunted. "Well, I'm glad to know I'm not alone."

"Most def not alone, Mad. Not sure it's good or bad. What's that saying? Something about misery loves company. Well, I'll sit back here horny as shit, and you sit up there thinking about me being horny."

"I'd offer to whip my dick out and jackoff for you while I drive if you did the same for me, but I'm afraid I'd crash us, and then it would be our luck the fucks chasing our asses would find us just as we were both ready to come." His snort endeared her.

He shifted in the seat, and she knew he was adjusting the erection in his jeans. "I'll take care of you when we get somewhere safe."

"Head down, Hales. Now!" Maddox kept his head straight, his voice tight as they drove.

Her heart rate kicked up to a furious beat.

"Coast is clear, but we are coming up to town. I'm going to continue through, but don't want you to get up until we are completely out of the city limits." As if he was listening to music, he tapped his fingers along the passenger seat. The action soothed her frayed nerves.

The time it took to drive through whatever town he'd driven them into seemed to take forever. Finally, he put his arm down, and looked around. "Okay, you can sit up. We're heading to a friend of a friend's place. He owns a security firm, and used to be a SEAL, too. He owes me a favor or two. I'll be calling one in."

Scraping her hair back from her face, she waited to see if he'd tell her who. "You gonna tell me who?"

"Sometimes, the less you know, the better."

Ominous words did not always make a person scared. In fact, she drew comfort from such things knowing he was only doing it to keep her safe. Hailey was a fierce fighter, and could handle herself in most situations, but she could admit when she was out of her league. Having someone try to kill you, and blow your shit up tended to make a gal realize she wasn't invincible.

"Mad, do you think JoJo and Blake are okay?" She worried her lower lip.

"Do you trust me?" he asked instead of answering.

She tilted her head to the side. "I wouldn't be in the back of god knows whose vehicle, going off somewhere that I have no clue where, if I didn't." She answered honestly.

"Then trust I wouldn't leave them unguarded."

Chapter Six

Maddox hated the uncertainty in the eyes staring back at him, but knowing nothing short of a call to the other men would wipe the look completely from her face. She may believe she trusted him completely, but something held her back to an extent. That inner alarm he admired in her that alerted her something wasn't as it seemed. Yeah, he was deceiving her, but not because he was out to kill her. She was truly safer with him than anywhere on the planet, in that he was sure. Had he not come upon her when he had, he wasn't sure what the plans for her would have been that day. Clearly they hadn't planned on killing her with those wild shots.

A shudder wracked him at the image of a broken and bloodied Hailey lying on that hill.

"We'll need to stop in a few hours and fuel up. It'll take us about eight hours to get to Omaha."

"Omaha," she repeated.

"Yep, like in Nebraska," he agreed.

"Why are we going there? That is almost middle freaking America for crying out loud." She looked around a bit wildly.

"Climb on up here, Hales. If you need to duck down, you can do it from up here." He patted the console. The last thing he wanted or needed was her worrying about their destination.

"Mad, I think we should just call our superiors. I mean if we up and leave without letting them know where we are, we could get into a lot of trouble."

"Hales, come up here." He used his don't argue with me tone, the one that made grown men stand at attention. It had the desired effect. His little hellion's back straightened.

"Don't think just because you are bigger than me, you are the boss all the time." However, she unsnapped the seatbelt, then maneuvered into the front of the vehicle.

He reached his hand over, placing it onto her thigh. "I don't think I'm the boss." He waited till she'd buckled back up. "I know I am. As for us getting into trouble, believe me when I say, you'd be in a lot more if you stayed in Rapid City. Now, since you're so worried, I want to point out that you were in an accident, and in the hospital. Both of which were reported. I took the liberty of filing the reports with the proper channels, and made sure that you were put on leave. Luckily for you, I was already on leave myself. Now, this is where you tell me how awesome I am." He squeezed her supple thigh.

"How, Maddox. Something is not adding up. I mean, I know I took a hit to the head. But this." She waved her hand around the vehicle. "Even for a SEAL, this seems a bit extreme for a non-operational assignment. Unless, I am one and wasn't aware of it." She crossed her arms over her chest, and stared at him.

He knew he'd have to explain, or make up another story, he just hadn't planned on doing it while on the road. Hell, he truly hadn't thought to be her guardian, yet here they were traveling across the country while he tried to figure out who was trying to kill her.

"I'll tell you everything you want to know when we get to Omaha. I promise, I'm one of the good guys." Although his conscience sometimes didn't agree. At the end of the day, they were saving more lives than they took.

"What about clothes and necessities?" she asked.

"We'll stop at a truck stop and get a few things there while we fuel up. This isn't forever, Hales. A day or two, and I'll have a better idea of where we need to go and what's going on." He winced as his side decided to shoot a stabbing pain down his leg.

"Damn it, Maddox. I told you to let me clean that up. Pull over and let me see it. We can't walk into a gas station, or anywhere with others if you've got blood all down your side." She reached for his shirt.

The black shirt and pants were a good camouflage for such injuries, but her words had merit. They'd been driving for well over two hours, and he figured they'd put at least a hundred miles between the cabin and themselves. Seeing a sign for a small town, he signaled to exit. A few turns, and he found a dirt road in the middle of nowhere.

"Let me grab the bag out of the back and get a fresh shirt."

She opened her door and followed him out. "I'll get the first aid kit out of the backseat."

The Bronco had a hatch that opened in the back, giving them plenty of room for storage. Maddox laughed as he got a look at the camping gear loaded inside.

"Damn, we are all set if we needed to become survivalists. FYI, I am not your girl for that. I like hot baths, electricity, and my lattes on the regular." Hailey sat the little white box down.

"Good to know." He eased his shirt up, the material sticking to the wound. The bullet had grazed him, creating a nice cut that had bled.

"Alright, big guy. This might sting a lot." She looked up at him, trepidation in her eyes.

"Go ahead. I can take it." He balled up the bloodied T-shirt and waited for her to apply the spray alcohol from the kit. The first hit had him flinching away but he ground his teeth, and held completely still while she cleaned him the best she could. And he knew she was doing a damn fine job by the fine sheen of sweat on her brow. "You're doing great, Hales," he reassured her.

A large piece of gauze was placed over the area, then taped off before she looked up at him. "I so was not cut out to be a nurse. I swear, I wanted to wrap my arms around you and say I was sorry like a hundred times."

The honesty of her words were like a punch to his solar plexus. No one had ever wanted to hug him because he was hurt before on a mission. Sure, Mike Royce, his partner, worried for his safety. They were partners, however, the thought of the other man giving him a hug because he'd had a scratch made him laugh.

"Awe, Hales. You have any clue what your words do to me?" He pulled her between his legs where he sat in the back of the Bronco. From their positions she was the perfect height for him to kiss without having to bend. A small taste that was all he wanted. Yet as soon as his lips touched hers, his body lit up. He ate at her mouth like a starving man, licking and biting until he realized they were in the middle of nowhere with people chasing them.

Easing back, he rested his forehead on hers. "Thank you for taking care of me."

"Right back atcha," she said impishly.

"Let's get back on the road. I want to hit Omaha before bedtime." Hell, he wanted to be between her supple thighs at bedtime, but thoughts like that were going to make it harder than hell to drive.

Her eyes went to the fly of his jeans, a grin tilted one side of her lips. "Dirty thoughts?"

"With you? Always." He hopped down from the back, and they worked to get the supplies put up, then were back on the road.

At the truck stop he decided to stop at, he pulled to the side and got out. His side gave a little throb. Hailey pulled her hair into a French braid, assuring him she never wore it like that. He gave her a flannel top out of the bag and laughed at the way she looked.

"Hey, I think I look quite lovely." She shook her ass at him.

In that moment, he couldn't agree more. Under those pants, he knew she had nothing on. Again, he had to pull his head out of the gutter. "Stay by my side, and don't make small talk with anyone. We'll grab something to eat and drink here. If you want some snacks, we'll get those too. Afterwards, we'll drive around to the other side where the store is and grab a few novelty things like we're tourists."

He put his arm around her waist as they entered, and together they walked down the aisles picking out a few treats. At the checkout, he paid for the entire lot, plus prepaid for enough gas to fill the tank.

"Dang, Daddy Warbucks. Where you get all that cash?" she asked once they were back inside and driving around to the store side.

"It was in the emergency bag." He looked around the lot. "Come on. Less time we spend here the better."

She sat up straighter and looked around. "Do you feel something is off?"

Taking a deep breath. "I'd just feel better if we weren't out in the open with a bunch of unknowns."

"We could skip this part and just wait until we reach Omaha." Her voice shook a little.

He parked in a spot that had an exit forward and backward. Knowing Hailey had her SIG, and he had his own weapons on him, he shook his head. "We'll be fine. In out, and on the road in under fifteen. Let's do this." He squeezed her hand, then hopped out, going around to her side to open the door.

"I know. Stay by your side. Remember, I am not a civilian, Mad," she protested as he put his arm around her.

He stared down at her, wishing like hell he could lock her inside the vehicle while he made the necessary purchases. "Which is why you are going along with me, instead of remaining in the Bronco. Try to avoid looking up as much as possible, and don't look directly at any cameras."

The bell above the door jingled. Except for the one woman manning the checkout, the store was empty. Shirts, hoodies, and even flannel pants with different characters in all sizes were what Hailey navigated toward. Her arms had several of each draped over them. He grabbed a couple ball caps, a few other things he thought they would need, and noticed Hailey eyeing a burner cellphone.

"Go ahead and add it to the pile," he instructed, taking the items from her arms and walking next to her as they approached the register.

At the counter, he silently applauded Hailey for her quick thinking as she dropped a shirt, and bending to pick it up, she turned to look back over the store, mouthing the word camera. He clenched his teeth. With the cap pulled down low over his eyebrows, he counted out the cash for their purchases. Instead of heading the correct direction on the highway toward Omaha, he made sure his vehicle was seen going the opposite direction. If their luck should happen to run out, and whoever was after Hailey could hack into the cameras with a facial recognition program, then they'd also be able to track them as they left. He explained to Hailey about the software that allowed you to be tracked, and how easy it was.

"I didn't even think of that. I mean I know of it, clearly. I just didn't think about it being used to locate me." She chewed on her thumb, then turned in the seat to stare at him. "You're not who you say you are, are you Maddox?" She held up her hand. "Don't feed me a line of bullshit. When you showed up over a year ago, the guys all thought you were a little too smooth to be Navy Intelligence like us. Hell, until the shit went down with Dex, I was sure we had a pretty boring job. I have a degree in computer science. I blend in with a crowd, and protect civilians when needed." She began ticking things off on her fingers. "I've given tactical support from afar, but more operational intelligence and civil maritime intelligence has fallen to others. The assignments with a scientific and technical focus, or that needed someone to analyze foreign weapons, those came to us. Hell, we even handle some human intelligence assignments, which is how we came to meet Kai and the SEAL Team Phantom. Of course when it came to face-to-face information collection, you were always sent in. Alone I might add. So, why don't you tell me the truth for a change, instead of the same bullshit you've been feeding us."

Maddox drummed his fingers on the steering wheel. "I told you I would explain everything when we get where we're going, Hales." He didn't bother looking at her.

"Damn it, you are pissing me off. What the fuck does it matter if you tell me now, or in another three or four hours?" Her voice raised, threatening to burst his eardrums.

Without taking his eyes off the wheel, he grabbed her hand. "It matters a whole hell of a lot. Now, settle down. I'm not the enemy here, Hales." He used more force than necessary to signal for the exit, wanting to turn back toward the right direction.

A quiet beep in his left ear alerted him to Royce wanting to talk to him. Fucking great! He exhaled loudly when Hailey kept her fingers entwined in his. Trying not to look obvious, he pressed the earbud.

"I'm so glad you decided to turn me back on, jackhole. How are things on your end? A grunt for good. Two grunts for bad and a snort for shut the fuck up Royce."

Maddox snorted at his partner's words.

"Going by your response, I'm going to assume you and the delectable Hailey are together and you can't talk. I'm also hoping I'm not interrupting any inserting of your part A, into her slot B time."

He barely restrained from growling at Royce. The man was an excellent CIA agent, but his twisted sense of humor tended to piss others off.

"Let me get something off my chest. Otherwise, I think I might implode. When we get to wherever the hell you are taking us, the first damn thing you best do, after we are settled, is explain." She gripped his fingers a little tighter with each word.

Knowing his partner, and best friend could hear every word, Maddox swore loudly.

"Surely, you aren't planning on telling her the whole truth, and nothing but the truth, so help you God?" Royce asked a squeak in his voice.

Hailey swore he waged some internal battle as she watched Maddox's face after she made her announcement. If the man continued to grind his teeth, they would be down to little nubs, but that was not her problem. She wanted...no, she corrected herself, she needed answers. Her feelings for him went a lot deeper than fellow soldier, or even lover. Hailey had fallen in lust with him the first time she'd seen him over a year ago. He'd walked into the building wearing his Navy uniform, looking way too comfortable in his surroundings, almost arrogant, but she still thought he was the sexiest thing she'd ever seen. He'd filled out the Navy slacks like none other, and his biceps were so large, she didn't think her hands would go all the way around them. However, all that would be a moot point if what he told her was something she couldn't live with.

With hundreds of miles left to go, she sat back and closed her eyes. The warmth of his hand still in hers not going unnoticed by either of them.

She jerked awake at the feel of the car coming to a stop, Maddox's hand still holding hers. "Are we there?"

He grinned, the dashboard lights highlighting his masculine features. "Yep. His left hand hung over the steering wheel as his eyes stared straight ahead."

A glance around, showed her a brick ranch with a huge tree in the front yard. "Where the hell are we?"

"This is where I grew up. Home I guess you could say."

His voice held a strange quality to it.

Night had fallen as she'd slept. She wondered if he had phoned ahead to tell his parents they were coming, but then they surely would have left a light on for them. The tire swing hanging from a branch looked like it hadn't seen much attention, yet the grass was freshly mowed and the home looked well-kept from the outside.

"Are we going in, or sitting out here all night?" She sat without moving.

"I'm going to pull into the garage." The driveway disappeared to the back of the house, revealing a three car attached garage with one door opening as they approached. Maddox released her hand once they'd cleared the entrance, shoving open his door. "I'll grab our supplies. I stopped about an hour ago and picked up some milk and a few other things from an all-night grocer."

"Dang, I must have been tired." A yawn caught her by surprise.

"You've been through hell. I'm shocked you haven't crashed before now." He hefted the bags from the backseat.

"I'll get the ones from the very back," she said, not giving him a chance to deny her.

She walked behind him up to the door, surprised to see the level of security on the old home. "Wow, your parents must be as security conscious as you."

Lights came on as they entered, the air had the scent of a vacant home.

Maddox went to the large fridge and put the milk and other supplies away while she silently waited. Without asking, she knew he was working up to telling her what she'd asked.

"Water?" he asked, holding a bottle of water in his hand.

She nodded, needing something to do.

"Let's go into the living room for this little chat, shall we." Maddox, ever the gentleman extended his hand for her to proceed him.

The typical ranch style home had an open floor plan from the kitchen to a large living room, with a huge picture window overlooking the front yard. More lights came on as they entered, yet not a speck of dust marred any surface of the place.

Patience wearing thin, she sat in the middle of the sofa hoping he'd sit next to her. Instead, he walked over to the fireplace.

"This was my home. See that tire swing out there?" He pointed toward the window with his bottle of water. "My mom and dad used to take turns pushing me in that when I was a kid." He took a deep breath. "You were right. I'm not in the Navy. My name is Maddox Lopez. I didn't lie about that. Hell, I think this is one of the first cases I've been able to use my real name."

The pain she saw in his eyes as he turned back to face her was like a knife to the gut. "Wait. Cases?"

"Hales, I work for the Central Intelligence Agency. We've long suspected someone on the inside has been selling out our agents, and their families to our enemies as leverage." He looked straight into the open area where a fire should have been. The hurt radiating off of him in waves.

"Your family?" she asked even though in her heart she knew.

"Five years ago someone showed up here and killed both my parents. Now, you might think it was some random murder, but I know the truth. My boss knows the truth. It was a professional hit, Hales. Do you want to know the details of how my mother was killed?" His knuckles turned white around the plastic.

She shook her head. "Do you think it was Dex who was leaking the information?" God, she couldn't fathom the pain he must've gone through. Nor, how Dex could have...

"No, I don't believe Dex is the mole, I believe he is just a small blip in the grand scheme of things."

"Damn it, Mad. You have got to be kidding me. I take a piss, and look what you go and do. Grow a fucking conscious," Royce growled. "Oh, yeah. SEAL Team Phantom is on their way, so try not to kill the friendlies."

"Fuck me running." Maddox pinched the bridge of his nose.

"What did I do?" She got off the couch, tired of sitting there while he stood apart from her.

He pointed to his ear. "My partner is talking to me."

Chapter Seven

Hailey stared at his ear, the tiny device unnoticeable. "That's incredible. So, can he hear me then?"

"Tell her I think she sounds sexy, and I wish I could see her."

"Royce, I will beat the shit out of you." Maddox touched the small device.

"You guys sound like you're close." She ran her hand up his arm. His muscles flexed under her palms, reminding her of his strength.

He swallowed audibly. "He's my best friend, more like a brother to me. I'd trust him with my life." He gave a dry laugh. "What am I saying? I have trusted him with my life on dozens of occasions. More importantly, I'd trust him with yours."

His head bent and he swooped down, taking her lips in a kiss that sent her senses reeling. His tongue swept in, tangling with hers, then glided along the seam of her lips. He tasted like peppermint gum. She truly could imagine running her tongue over his for the next hundred years, and never get tired.

A cry escaped from her as he pulled her body flush with his, and moved to kiss her neck. Her eyes drifted open, every muscle in her body strung tight in anticipation.

Lights flicking off in the distance had her jerking against him. "Maddox, I think a car just turned its lights off at the end of the drive."

His fingers stilled on her breast. Calm settled over his features. His jaw firmed.

"Royce, I've got company. Where you at, buddy?" Maddox moved them away from the window, his hand wound around her elbow, securing her to his side.

She would fight with him. "What's the plan? Is Royce near?"

"He's not answering me." They went back to the kitchen while he began pulling weapons out of the bag.

"Shit. Did they follow us? How could they follow us?" Hailey looked around wildly. One minute she was making out with Maddox, thinking how much she wanted to make love to him, and the next they were loading up with weapons.

He looked up from where he was checking ammo. "Do you have anything on you from home?" His lips turned down, his eyes taking her in like she was the prey.

Black leggings and the shoes on her feet were hers, everything else were borrowed, or new, which she pointed out.

There was a slight hardening of his eyes. "I'm such a dumbass. If I was going to put a tracer on someone, I'd put it on something they don't change every damn day." He raised his finger. "For a female that would be her purse, phone, backpack in your case, and for a universal object or article do you know what it would be?" He laughed mirthlessly, then pointed at her shoes. "Your fucking shoes."

She tried to step forward, but his angry shake of his head stopped her. "I need to get you to the basement. There is a bunker down there. Although, there isn't an escape route like the last place, you'll be safe there until help arrives."

Like hell. He planned to stay up here and fight whoever, and however many came at them while she hid in a corner. Not happening.

"Listen, you aren't thinking clearly. We don't know how many are out there, nor do we know who. They are obviously wanting something they think I have, right? So it would make sense for you to go be scarce, while I stay up here and face what comes at us."

Of course his little hellion, standing there explaining how she wanted to be the one to take on the bad guys turned him on, and made him fucking nuts. He wasn't sure what to do or say that wouldn't piss her off, other than to shake his head in instant denial.

"I can't lose you, Hales." He shifted, taking her with him away from any of the windows. The hallway to the bedrooms was the only area where they were afforded that privacy. Although he had installed security and replaced all the furniture after his parent's murders, he hadn't thought he'd need to do more upgrades to the home. The bunker in the basement was installed years ago when he'd first become an agent.

He fucking hated being the hunted, when he'd always been the one doing the hunting. "I need to cut the power. When I had the house refurbished...after. I wanted to make sure if anyone entered, the lights would come on in any room you entered. That makes us a visible target."

"I'll stay up here and watch the doors. Can you shut the power off without turning off the alarms?" Her eyes darted down the hall. Outwardly calm, he could see a pulse beating in her slim throat.

He put his finger under her chin, stopping her motions. "Yeah. The alarm is on a backup system. Keep your eyes and ears open. Shoot first and ask questions later." Giving her a quick kiss, he strode back toward the living room and down the stairs to the basement.

Within moments the lights were out, pitch black swallowed him and the surrounding area. If he hadn't played video games and hide and seek as a kid down there, he might have been worried. Snaking his way back up the steps, he let the small bit of light from the outside be his guide. The almost silent beep in his ear gave him hope Royce was back online. He was locked in silence since he didn't want to speak in case someone else had the earpiece on the other end.

A fist reached out of the darkness, catching him off guard and knocked him into the wall. A stubborn will lit deep within him. He could make out two shadowy figures. The one fighting him, and another working his way around the center island.

Maddox let his voice rise. "What the hell were you doing, waiting inside for us all this time? Why didn't you show your faces instead of waiting till the lights went out, pussies?"

The man in front of him brought up his booted foot and kicked, missing Maddox by a half an inch. A stirring of air behind him, and then a glimmer of light showed a predatory smile cross the face of Dex in front. Maddox didn't stop to think, he dropped to the ground, reaching for the gun tucked into the ankle holster he always kept. A single shot rang out, as he rolled away from whoever was behind him.

His gut tightened at the sound of a heavy thud hitting the ground.

"Shit, you shot me." Dex's pain filled voice came out garbled.

Maddox kept his back to the island, easing around the solid surface, listening for any sound of movement. The fact he hadn't heard Hailey make any noise sent his inner caveman into overdrive. The small gun was pointed off to the side, while he pulled the Glock from the back of his pants. With both guns held at the ready, he made his way back to where he'd left his heart. If anything happened to her, he'd go on a rampage like nothing before.

The moon shone a beam of light on the tile between the area he was and where he needed to be. With his breathing even, he began to lift from his crouched position.

"I told you, I don't know anything. I wasn't part of that team." Hailey's voice sounded closer than it should have.

"Your friend Dex begged to say different. For a few million dollars, he told me and my employer you would tell us where we could find Jase Tyler. Now, if you want to continue to breathe, I suggest you come with me. And you, Maddox Lopez. Clearly, I have your girlfriend. Unless you want to die like the idiot on your kitchen floor, I suggest you let me take the girl."

Maddox's throat worked up and down as bile threatened to come up. He couldn't lose Hailey. If she left with whoever the man with the monotone voice was, she'd be gone from him forever.

"So what's it gonna be, soldier boy." The man asked, acting like a shark playing with the small fish in the ocean before he gobbled them up.

His whole body tensed as he waited for the man to step into the beam of light. Prayed for that one shot.

"Don't do it, Mad. Kai and his team are here. They want that man alive. I know you want to tell me to fuck off, but the man he is searching for used to be on their team. He betrayed them, and almost got them all killed or some shit." Royce spoke slowly and quietly, never a good thing.

"Why do you want this Tyler so much?" He wasn't entirely convinced all wasn't as it seemed on Royce's end. His partner had gone quiet for too long during a mission. Something they never did unless the other was injured or doing extracurricular things. The latter Maddox knew Royce wouldn't be doing at this point in time.

A nasty laugh met his questions. "Do you think this is like the movies where you get me to talk, and someone on the other end of some recording device will hear my nefarious plans? Get real."

Just a few more steps and he was sure Hailey and whoever was holding her would be within his sites. "Hales, you okay?"

"I'm fine, Maddox. I can't see anything though. He sort of came out of nowhere and put a black thing over my face, and had me restrained quicker than I like to admit." She gritted out.

The image of the guy ambushing her, and what he could have done had he wanted to kill her made his blood run cold.

There was a sound of something thudding, and then a feminine moan of pain. He had to stay where he was even as it ate at his soul.

"If your girl tries to run again, I'll put a bullet in her leg."

His jaw clenched at the matter of fact way he spoke.

The front door exploded open, giving Maddox the opening he'd been waiting for. Impotent rage threatened to choke him as he rushed the distance between them. Whoever was coming through the door offered the distraction he needed. Silent thuds, only a gun with a silencer made, made sheetrock fly near his head. His arm jerked as a bullet found him in the dark, but it didn't stop him from his target.

Lights lit up the living room and hall as Kai and his team came in with guns blazing. Maddox ignored them, stalking back toward the room he could see little specks of blood leading to now that there were lights.

"Stand down, Lopez," Kai yelled.

He felt a hand on his shoulder and twisted the owners arm. "Don't make me break this, boy. You may need it again." Letting go he rushed into the room completely devoid of furniture.

Kai blinked at him, but signaled they'd follow. Maddox gave no fucks at that moment, knowing the other man had Hailey.

The nondescript man was someone he'd never seen, and wasn't sure he'd recognize if he'd passed again. The patio doors leading out were open, with the security lights from outside giving them enough room to see the man.

Hailey's head was still covered and with her hands in zip ties behind her back, she stumbled behind the man.

"You might as well stop running. There is no way you'll get out of here alive, even with the girl as a shield." He stated calmly.

The lines of the man's face became hard, that of a stone cold killer. "I already made my deal with the devil. Have you? You see, I knew going in this could be a one way ride." He raised his gun before Maddox realized what he planned to do and shot himself in the head.

"Motherfuckingsonofabitch," Kai gasped, rushing over to the falling body.

Maddox hurried over to pull Hailey away from the dead man. "I'm taking Hailey back to the living room. I need to call this in."

"Mad, get this fucking thing off me." Hailey struggled against him.

She'd been so calm he hadn't thought anything of the hood covering her, only wanted to get her away from the blood and gore that was left of the other man.

"Easy, love. Let me." He had to use a knife to cut the strings holding the ends in a knot, then pulled the offending thing off.

Wild dark eyes stared around like a frightened animal. "Is he dead?"

He nodded. "Oh god, is that his blood on me?" She looked at her shoulder and cringed.

"I'm sorry, Hales. Let's go get you cleaned up." He led her into the bathroom across the hall. The SEAL named Oz stared at him. At six foot three, the big red haired man probably intimidated many with his fierce size. Yet the one named Sully, with his dark skin and piercing green eyes, had what he and Royce referred to as 'the looking at you like they'd done killed you ten times in their head stare.' Not that he was worried.

The overhead lights came back on, giving some relief to the darkness. Before she could get a glimpse at the mess on her shirt, he grabbed the front and ripped it in two. The action causing the wound in his arm to make him curse. "Damn it. I've been shot more in the last forty-eight hours than I have in the last year."

She looked down at her chest, then up at him. "That was kind of sexy."

"You ain't got time for shower sex, Mad. I've got a room full of SEALs ready to take my head off, so I'm gonna need you to get to getting, and get out here ASAP," Royce said with his ever present humor.

"Do you ever want to throat punch him?" Hailey asked with a straight face.

He nodded. "So many times it hurts."

A loud knock interrupted them again. "I brought your girl a change of clothes I found in the kitchen." Royce's voice faded. "You're welcome by the way."

"Let the throat punching commence later. He has clean clothes for me. Now, I just need some shower supplies and I'm good, but I'll take warm water." Hailey turned toward the shower and started it.

He opened the door to find the pile of clothing and a small shower kit. Royce was good for a few things.

"Oh, bless him. I will kiss him instead of hit him."

"How about you shower quickly, and kiss me later." He swatted her ass as she shimmied out of her clothing and got into the steaming water.

They walked back out to find Royce standing near the fireplace where he'd stood only a short time ago dressed all in black, while the men he'd met while pretending to work for the Navy stood glaring at him.

"Has Royce told you anything of importance?"

"If you mean has he explained who the hell you were, then the answer is no. Has he showed us his middle finger repeatedly, then yes? If I didn't think I'd be in a shitload of trouble, I'd show him what he could do with that finger," Kai growled.

Royce raised his dark brows. He and Kai could almost pass for brothers, only Royce had about forty pounds of muscle on the SEAL. Not to mention the fact his partner was deadly with or without a gun.

Once he got confirmation from Royce that they could share a little information about their mission, he could see each man become more rigid.

"So, Dex was just in it for the money?" Kai blew out a frustrated breath.

Hailey nodded. "He told them I knew more, which is a lie. I don't know if he thought he could get more money out of them, or what. I think he's the one who tried to kill me and either got scared, or had a bit of a second thought at the last minute. He truly wasn't the greatest shot on the best days." Although she knew he'd tried to kill her, it still hurt to know one of the men she'd worked with for years would barter with her life.

"CIA, I never would have pegged you for that. I mean, shit." Coyle shook his head.

Maddox shrugged. "That's good. It's not like we walk around with it on our shirts. This is classified information." He stumbled a little.

"Hey, I think he might need some medical attention." Kai grabbed him before he fell.

Hailey was on his other side. "Sit down before you fall down."

"Only because I think you may be right," he muttered allowing them to lead him to the leather sofa.

"Well, shit. Looks like we'll be taking you to the hospital. Can't have you passing out on us. Load em up boys." Kai clapped his hands.

Maddox squinted up. "I just need to rest a few."

"He's probably lost too much blood from being shot twice and neither time did anything but grunt and keep moving." Hailey glared at him.

Royce pushed away from the fireplace. "Damn, always gotta be the tough one. Alright, let's do this."

Between Royce and Oz they maneuvered him into the Bronco with Hailey sitting next to him. They looked like their own little convoy as they headed back into town, leaving his family's home once again with death and bodies inside.

"I'll make sure it's closed up and properly cleaned," Royce said from the front seat.

Maddox looked at the brick ranch and shook his head. He couldn't imagine ever coming back there to visit, let alone live. He'd make sure the government got rid of the property quietly.

The way the men all got out, setting up a defensive perimeter had the good folks of Omaha's General Hospital gaping at them. Maddox could only imagine what they probably looked like with several of them in camo, while he and Royce were all in black.

A quick call to the right people, and they were rushed through without incident.

"Damn, being CIA must be nice." Oz leaned against the wall.

Glaring at the men who didn't seem in any hurry to leave, Maddox lifted his middle finger. "Don't you have a ship to be on or some shit?"

Sully shook his head. "Nah, we are good on air, land, and sea. Besides, we're your protection detail until you're released."

Hailey smiled. "I think I like that."

"Hales, come here." He held his hand out. Imagining her with the other man had him seeing red.

"What's wrong? Are you hurting?" She ran her hand over his head.

"Oh, I know that look. Boys, I think we should step outside." Royce motioned toward the door.

Chapter Eight

It had been over a month since Dex had been killed and she'd seen Maddox. Hailey wasn't sure what to think, other than he'd changed his mind. After the other men had left the hospital room he'd told her to give him a kiss. Then, when she'd tried to pull away, he'd explained she was his. Nobody else's but his. Her heart had skipped a beat, and she'd said it went both ways. His hand had went to the back of her neck and held her so they were looking eye to eye. His growled words of *only his* and *of course he was hers*, had her covering his mouth with a soft cry. If she could have, she'd have climbed onto the bed with him as the heat had exploded between them. Royce's knock to let them know he was being discharged was the only thing that kept her, and him, from acting on the impulse.

She sat back with a heavy sigh. Maybe it was time to go home. Her family surely wouldn't roll out all the words of wisdom they thought she needed, and ones she hated, since she wasn't returning with what they'd call a failure. Her latest enlistment was up. She could move home and start a new life. A life without half her heart. She snorted and turned her computer on. The words on the screen didn't make sense to her, something that never happened in her line of work as a computer science expert.

Standing, she went to the wall of windows overlooking Rapid City. Far below she could see people milling about their day, while she felt like her own life was stuck on the hamster wheel. "Time to hop off and quit with the spinning," she admonished herself.

"I don't know, I kind of like it when you're on top. Well, in my fantasies that is."

She spun at the sound of Maddox's deep voice coming from behind her. He made her breath catch. "What are you doing here?"

Dressed in a pair of denim jeans and a polo shirt, she couldn't remember ever seeing him look better. Every part of her wanted to run into his arms and beg him to hold her, and never let go.

"I came to see you." Maddox's eyes went from her head to her toes, making her glad she'd worn one of her best dresses.

Taking a deep breath. "Oh." What the hell did he want her to say? It had been thirty-three days, sixteen hours and a handful of minutes since she'd seen or heard from him, but she wasn't keeping count.

"Can I come in?" he asked.

"Of course." She gestured to the seat in front of her desk. The cubicles outside her office showed several heads above them staring at her and Maddox.

"I think they're curious as to why I'm here." He pointed his thumb backward.

His grin did funny things to her belly. "I believe the story was you were injured and released from active duty. You being here looking as healthy as any of us sort of makes that seem odd." She took a fortifying breath. "What are you doing here, Maddox?"

He waited until he had the door shut, then went around and closed the blinds, blocking the view from the others. By the time he finished her nerves were strung tight.

"Why do you think I'm here, Hales?" His tone deepened, and then he was walking around her desk, coming to a stop in front of her.

With her left hand holding her desk, and the right gripping her chair, she stared at the man she loved beyond reason. "Why don't you tell me."

He pinched her chin between his thumb and forefinger. "You're going to make me grovel aren't you?"

Licking her lips she waited.

A growl escaped him. "I fucking love you. I loved you the moment I walked in to this operation thinking one of you were a traitor, and plans started forming of how I'd get you out if it was you. When I saw you on the side of the road and the shit hit the fan, my heart nearly stopped. For the last month I've worked my ass off to get a plan in motion so I could offer you something other than a nomadic life. You deserve more than a man who leaves for weeks, months at a time without notice. I didn't want to start a life with you, and make promises I couldn't keep. One that I couldn't guarantee I'd not come home to. I resigned from my job."

She couldn't believe her ears. Knowing Maddox and the way he'd been, imagining him as anything other than what he was didn't compute. "Why?" The one word question came out a hoarse whisper.

"I can't live without my heart and soul. You are it for me, Hellion." He didn't give her a chance to say anything else. The small space he'd allowed was eliminated by him as his arms snaked around her, lifting her off her feet, bringing her flush to his body.

In that moment she cursed the form fitting dress and her inability to wrap her legs around his waist. When they broke apart they were both panting. "I love you so much it hurts, Mad. For the last month, my world was cold and empty without you. I think JoJo and Blake were ready to hunt you down and either kill you, or hogtie your ass until you came back."

Her arms were locked around his neck, hands smoothing over his shaved head. God, she loved everything about this man.

Maddox laughed. "I'd like to see that."

"I'm sure they'd reenact their plans for us if you'd like." She laughed down at him.

Maddox's hands smoothed up her thighs, taking the skirt of her dress with them. He sat her on the top of the desk once he'd lifted it to her waist. "I need you, Hales."

"Oh god, yes."

The phone on her desk rang with the shrill tone that indicated an inner office call. She pressed her forehead to his chest. "That would be my boss."

He tugged on the hair at the back of her head. "You should answer it then." Fire danced in his dark eyes.

She slipped the headset on over her head. "Hailey here."

"I see you've got a visitor. Why don't you take the rest of the afternoon off?" Amusement laced her director's voice.

"Thank you, Sir." Hailey took the device off, then repeated what was said.

"How long before you can leave?" His fingers traced the seam of her panties.

Her hand covered his. "Right now."

He took a step back, helping her get off her desk and ease the dress back into place. "Let's go then."

After shutting down her computer, she opened a drawer on her desk and pulled out her crossbody bag.

"Where's your backpack?" he asked looking at her with a curious expression.

"I only carry it when I ride my bike." She touched his arm at the look of pain that crossed his face.

Maddox screwed his eyes shut, a shudder wracked him. "Don't remind me. How did you get to work today?" Moving around the desk he loved watching the way she glided around the small space, like a graceful ballerina. Damn, he had it bad.

"I caught a ride with JoJo and Blake. Did you drive here?" She came to stand in front of him.

"Does a bear shit in the woods?" He smiled.

Shaking her head, she tapped a message into her phone. "Alright, they are informed."

"Good," he said then scooped her into his arms, making her gasp.

"What are you doing?" she asked, her head turning toward the door as they stepped into the hall.

He laughed at the shocked expression on her face. "I believe it's romantic for a man to sweep his woman off her feet and carry her off. There's even a movie where the hero does it, and everyone cheers as he carts her off to the stunned disbelief of all those around."

Her laughter had many standing up to see what was happening. "That was An Officer and a Gentleman, and he was the Navy pilot, while she was a local girl out to catch herself a husband."

He looked down. "Same concept, Hales. Only I hope to catch myself a Navy girl to be with me."

Hailey's arms around his neck, and then her head nuzzling his throat had him sporting wood as he carried her through the building, but as the saying goes, he gave no fucks. With the woman in his arms, he truly would make an ass of himself every day if it meant she'd be with him.

"Take me away, Maddox, I'm yours to do with as you please," she said into his ear.

"Wait till I get you to my hotel suite, and I'll have you repeat that." He licked the shell of her ear.

The ride to his hotel was the longest he'd ever made, but with Hailey's hand securely in his, he made it in less than ten minutes. He handed the valet the keys, then walked swiftly to the bank of elevators, barely saying a word to Hailey. If he stopped to look at her, he feared he'd kiss her. If he began kissing, then they may end up getting arrested for public indecency. The one thing he did do was hold her hand in his. If he could, he'd have her handcuffed to him for the next fifty years or so.

"You know, Maddox, if I didn't feel your love so strongly, I'd be worried at your silence," Hailey murmured from beside him at the door to his suite.

The light turned green, and then he was ushering them inside. As soon as the door shut behind them, he had her against the wall. "Fuck, that was the longest fourteen minutes of my life," he groaned against her mouth.

His fingers found the zip on the side of the dress, and worked it down. "Need you, Hales."

Her breath was ragged, but she nodded. The dress slithered to the floor, leaving her in a cream colored bra and white panties.

"Hey, only women planning to get laid wear matching bra and panties every day." She put her hands on slim hips.

Maddox shook his head. "I love you. These need to go. They offend me."

A quick flick of his fingers and the bra was added to the pile of clothes, followed closely by the scrap of silk and lace. Standing in nothing but the spiked heels, he let his gaze eat her up. For over a month he'd done nothing but think of her, wishing she was next to him day in and day out.

"You are even more gorgeous than I remember." His index finger traced one pink nipple, watching it harden under his ministrations.

"You're a little overdressed."

Needing to kiss and lick every inch of her, he brought his mouth down over hers, his hands smoothed down her back, then lifted her. He began walking into the suite, past the living area into the bedroom. He heard two thuds and knew she'd kicked off the shoes. "We'll rectify my state of dress shortly."

He felt like a teenage boy with his first woman, ready to come in his jeans at any moment. Her slight weight was nothing to him, but he needed his hands free to do all the things he wanted.

"Show me what you got, big boy."

Her impish grin made his entire body come alive even more. "Oh, I think you know what I got." Maddox put her on the bed and had his shirt over his head in a heartbeat. He pushed his jeans and shoes off seconds later, naked as she was, standing with his hands on his hips next to the bed. "How is that for what I got, Hales?" His voice sounded a couple of octaves lower to his own ears.

She licked her lips, getting up onto her knees, one hand reaching for him. "Beautiful," her voice smooth and sweet like the finest whiskey he'd ever drank, pouring over him like a warm blanket.

"Touch me," he ordered.

Hailey didn't hesitate, her fingers encircling his shaft. With a sweet little smile, she swept her thumb over the slit and the small bead of come on the tip.

He held still under her intense gaze, waiting to see what she'd do. Hailey was by far the most complex woman he'd ever known. She was gorgeous, smart, kinky, sexy as all get out, and the most loyal woman he'd ever met. She'd take a bullet for her friends, and wouldn't think twice about offering the shirt off her back to someone in need. Maddox needed to let her know he would be right there with her, making sure all her wants and needs were satisfied.

His eyes nearly rolled to the back of his head as she bent and took the head of his cock into her warm mouth. She pulled back, giving the tip an oddly innocent kiss. He brushed her lips with the head, the pushed back inside.

Her hands shook while she ran her tongue along the length of him, a little moan of pleasure adding to his own came from her throat.

"That feels good, Hellion." His voice interrupted the quiet of the room, but there was no mistaking the husky truth.

His heart filled as she peered up at him. He could see she loved him as much as he loved her.

"Suck me harder, love."

She leaned forward, taking him back inside and sucked on the head of his dick. Watching her take him inside her mouth was a thing of true beauty. Her graceful back with her hair hanging loose, and the sight of her gorgeous ass, all combined to have him close to coming.

He felt a drop of pearly fluid pulse out, and her tongue lick at the slit, a hum of approval at his salty taste had him gripping her by the back of her head.

"Damn, Hales."

Hailey sucked, drawing his cock all the way to the back of her throat. Her right hand cupped his balls while she worked him with her lips, tongue and teeth.

The last thing he wanted was for their first time in over a month to end with him coming down her throat. He eased back with a groan she echoed.

His cock stood straight out, begging for her attention.

Hailey's eyes roamed him from head to cock and back. "You okay, Mad?"

He climbed onto the bed, pushing her to the middle as he went. "More than okay. I'm with the woman of my dreams." He kissed her neck, then moved down to her perfect pink and brown nipples making sure to be gentle with them. He licked each, then sucked on them softly. His fingers trailed down her stomach, finding her wet and soft. Kneeling between her thighs, he sank two fingers inside. "I've missed this. Missed you." He curled his fingers, finding her G-spot.

"God, yes, right there." Hailey worked her hips back and forth.

Maddox couldn't stand waiting another minute. He pulled his fingers out, licking them clean, watching her eyes flare as she tracked his movements. He ripped open a condom he'd left on the end table next to the bed. Years of practice had him rolling the latex on in record time, and then he was lining his cock up next to her entrance.

She took his breath away, raising her arms in welcome, her body made perfectly for him.

He stared down, fully focusing on the place where their bodies were joining. "Now, that is a pretty sight," he gritted out. He loved watching his dick stretch her, filling her paler flesh with his hard darker one, making himself a part of her. "You're so fucking tight." The words were ground out.

She sank her nails into his back. "You feel amazing." She breathed out as he fucked back into her.

In a low guttural voice, he told her how good she felt stretched around him. Each time he pushed back in, she pressed up to meet his thrusts. They found a perfect rhythm that had them both racing for that magic place.

Every movement of her tight body brought him closer as she fucked him with total abandon, seeking her own pleasure with as much need and passion as him. "Need you to come with me, Hales." Maddox couldn't contain the hunger rising to the surface. He pushed up onto his hands, his pelvis hitting her clit on each downward thrust. The orgasm just out of reach rushing closer.

She cried out, her body stiffened beneath his, then she shook as she came, crying out his name. Without hesitation, he followed her into bliss, allowing the orgasm he'd held at bay to flow out of him.

"Fucking love you, Hales. I'll cuff you and claim you as mine, so you might as well agree to marry me," he muttered against her neck.

Hailey had to take a moment to catch her breath. Her heart pounded in her ears, satisfaction invaded her languorous body. Maddox lay half on her, half off. His declaration hung in the air. Was she dreaming, or had he just proposed to her.

His hands flexed on her stomach, his head came up and she stared into his gorgeous eyes. "Did you just ask me to marry you?"

"If you want to consider it me asking instead of me telling?" He gave a lazy grin.

She smoothed her hand over his head. "Maddox Lopez, you are the only man who could make a proposal sound like a demand." Only it was one she could totally get on board with. "Since you are no longer gainfully employed, how are you going to do that?" she asked. A smile of love and pure pleasure racing over her.

"Sweetheart, I said I no longer worked for the alphabet company, I didn't say I was unemployed. That is what took me so long to come back. I needed to make sure it was ready to roll."

Maddox groaned then rolled out of the bed. "Let me get rid of this and I'll be right back."

She watched him disappear, then realized she wouldn't have to do that ever again. Well, not the way she had.

"What's put that smile on your face?" he asked walking back in uncaring of his nudity.

Shaking her head, she held her hand out. "I was just enjoying the view of you leaving and coming back."

He let his hands wander down her body. "You have the most deliciously curvy ass, and a brain to boot. I can't wait to spend the rest of my life worshipping it."

"Care to tell me about what you'll be doing and where?"

Hailey listened to him explain how he and Royce had opened a private security firm a couple years back with a partner who had been running things in Texas. She narrowed her eyes at him. "So, you're moving to Texas?"

"I was hoping we'd move to Texas after your term, if you wanted. Or I'd go wherever you went. I'm pretty mobile. Royce has already taken up residence down at the home office, but we will take on clients all over the states who need help with security."

Listening to him talk about his new venture, her mind raced with how she could help. With her computer skills, and his, along with their other knowledge in the field, she could easily see them having a great future. "I'm all in. That still doesn't explain how you can cuff me to your side."

A wicked gleam lit his brown eyes. Reaching over her body, he pulled the drawer out and showed her a badge and held up a pair of handcuffs. "Every private detective has to have a set of these, baby."

She laughed at his outrageousness. Being cuffed and claimed by Maddox Lopez was truly the best thing to ever happen to her.

The End

Bodhi's Synful Mate

Iron Wolves MC Book 6

"I swear to the fucking Goddess. If I see that wolf texting or talking on that motherfucking phone one more fucking time all secretive like, I'm gonna lose my shit." Syn glared at the bar watching Bodhi turn away with his phone pressed to his ear. Again. Her best friend Lyric who was standing next to her, was smart enough to turn her head away and cough into her hand, yet Syn knew she was laughing. Sometimes being a wolf sucked. "Fucking wolf hearing. Doesn't the man know I can hear him even when he's whispering?"

Lyric put her hand on Syn's arm. "I'm sure it's not what it sounds like."

She looked down at her best friend's hand and tried really hard not to growl. They'd been friends since they were little. Hell, Syn couldn't remember a day when they hadn't been. However, staring at them, they looked like night and day. Lyric had wavy blonde hair and brown eyes and was cute as a button. Where she had black hair and blue eyes. Growing up, she'd envied Lyric's gorgeous blonde locks, and dark eyes. Her petite form made her stand out, unlike Syn who was an average five foot five. Her real name was Karsyn, but went by Syn, another thing she loved about Lyric, her name was awesome without having to shorten it.

"Oh sure, and rainbows are flying out of his ass, too." Syn's eyes watched Bodhi stomp through the backdoor of the Iron Wolves club. Hell, even that was a gorgeous sight.

"Don't do anything crazy, Syn. You know Kellen would gladly woop his ass if you asked." Lyric raised her hand to get Turo's attention.

"What can I get you, gorgeous?" Turo leaned down on his muscular forearms against the smooth bar, his tattoos flexing.

The scent of peppermint wafted across the counter. Lord how she wished she didn't want Bodhi the porchdick, and could want this wolf instead. She licked her lips as she stared at him.

Turo shook his head. "Ain't happening, Sugar. That wolf would rip my head off." He winked.

Syn pouted up at Turo. "Awe, come on Arturo. You've got that big ole gun. You can totally shoot his ass for me."

Lyric smacked her in the arm. "Why you gotta bring up *the gun?*"

Syn laughed at Lyric's whispered words. Lyric had busted up Turo's favorite AR-15 in a bar fight against a rival pack, Rowan had replaced the weapon, but the big man swore it didn't shoot right. She rolled her eyes, and tried to ignore the pain in her chest at the sight of Bodhi walking out of the bar. The feeling was like a knife in her chest. She needed to get away. Far, far away, but she had to do it without the pack knowing, or they'd never allow her to leave. Hell, having her brother be the big bad alpha had its perks, but it had a lot of downs as well.

"Alright, bottoms up." Lyric handed her a shot glass.

One glance at the milky liquid, and she smiled. Her best friend had a thing for the alcohol called RumChata. "Bottoms up," Syn echoed before clinking her glass against Lyric's then draining the sweet concoction. "Turo, line em up, and keep em coming."

The way his eyebrows shot up would've been comical if he'd not have glanced behind them, asking for permission from one of the menfolk if it was okay. Yeah, she so fucking needed to get the hell outta Dodge, and away from nosy ass wolves.

"If you want, I can go elsewhere." It wasn't an empty threat. Although Lyric was happily mated and wouldn't be going with her, she'd gladly go to a human bar and get her drink on. Turo sighed, then refilled their drinks. Their shifter metabolism would burn off the alcohol quicker than a human, but they'd at least get tipsy if they drank quickly, and enough. She planned to do both.

"You gonna tell me what's going on in that head of yours?" Lyric turned to face her, the no nonsense tone saying more than just the words.

She shook her head. "Not tonight. I just want to drink and dance. Maybe see who's beating the shit out of who in the cages."

Yeah, watching a few shifters in their skin, shirtless, would definitely cheer her up.

Lyric snorted. "Good luck with that. I think the only thing that would do the trick, would be if someone hauled that dumb wolf into the ring and beat some sense into him."

Just the mention of Bodhi made her wolf whine inside her head. Turo refilled their drinks again. She looked at the sweet looking drink, but no longer felt like drinking.

"You know, I think I'll just head home. Would you mind if I took a raincheck on our girls' night?" Taking a look over her shoulder, she could see Rowan was standing next to Kellen and his mate Laikyn. She loved her brother and new sister-in-law, but watching the way neither could keep their hands off each other, brought home the fact all of her family and closest friends were happily mated. Except her. The proverbial third wheel. Fuck! She was not going to be a pity party for one, thank you very much. Even from the distance of fifty feet, the heat of Rowan's stare toward Lyric, was enough to melt a block of ice.

"Oh come on, the night is young," Lyric protested.

She pushed the shot glass toward Lyric. "Here, drink up and go have some fun with that man of yours. I'm gonna go home and catch up on some Netflix. Watching all y'alls make googly eyes at each other makes a girl wanna gag," she said with a laugh, inserting just enough truth so Lyric wouldn't scent a lie.

Her best friend wrapped her arms around Syn. "I love you. You know that right? No matter what. You and I will always be bestest friends forever."

Of course they would, but a mate came before friends. She knew that. Understood it even. However, she and her wolf were getting damn tired of fighting the pull of being without her own mate, even though she'd known who he was since she was fifteen. Syn was ready to try the whole *distance makes things easier* motto. When Lyric had mated Rowan, she'd gone to their place with the intention of leaving then, but couldn't work up the courage at the time. Now, with everyone else paired off, Xan with Breezy, Kellen with Laikyn, it was time for her to make a move. Had Bodhi been born a shifter instead of turned as a child, maybe he wouldn't be able to ignore her the way he'd been. Maybe he wouldn't be pursuing whoever he was on the phone twenty-four hours a day, seven days a week. The thought had her wolf growling, clawing to get out. She fought her back, not wanting Lyric to see how close she was to losing her shit.

"I'll give you a call. We can meet at the new coffee shop and see if their lattes are as good as our favorite place. Heck, it looks really cute from the outside." She got up and put a twenty dollar bill on the counter. "Keep the change, Turo." Before anyone could say a word, she turned and walked out the side door.

The cold night air whipped around her, sending a shiver down her spine. Her ears picked up the low timber of Bodhi speaking to someone in the distance. With it only being his voice she heard, it was easy to deduce he was on his cell. Realizing she couldn't and wouldn't stick around to listen to him talk to another female, she climbed into her pickup. A single tear fell from her eye before she swiped it away. "Fuck him. I don't need him," she whispered as she started the engine. The need to kick up some gravel had her foot twitching, but she pushed it back.

Always pushing her wolf back, Syn shifted the truck into gear, easing from the packed lot. Friday nights were always busy at the Iron Wolf, but with it being winter it was more so.

She made the short trip to her small cabin, music blaring while she made up her mind. No way could she continue to beat her heart against a wall and stay happy. Had she not been a wolf, she could go find another man and fuck Bodhi out of her system. However, since she'd been fifteen and come to know who her mate was, her wolf wouldn't allow her to get that close to another male. The bitch, Syn cursed the wolf living inside her. As she sat and looked at the small cabin she'd made her own, tears fell unheeded from her eyes. The porch had a swing on one side, and two Adirondack chairs on the other with a small table between them. She'd lovingly bought them, hoping one day to sit out there with her mate and watch the sunset together. Hell, she'd hoped Bodhi and she would sit out there together.

"Put your big girl panties on, and get your shit together." She swiped the backs of her hands across her cheeks, wiping away the evidence of her weakness. No sense crying over spilled milk as the saying went.

Once inside the cabin, she didn't bother turning on any lights. Able to see with her shifter abilities, she went straight to her bedroom and grabbed the bag she'd packed two months prior. Kneeling on the floor inside her closet, she dialed the lock, opening the small safe bolted to the floor, and took out her emergency funds. If she planned to have a little break from the pack, she'd have to go off the grid, meaning she'd have to do it with cash. Kellen would track her ass through her credit cards, but she'd been planning on a little trip alone for over a year. Hell, she'd been squirreling away cash for the last five if she was honest. After making sure the cabin was locked up, and the note explaining she was taking a little road trip, alone, she placed it and her cellphone on the counter. She'd pick up a burner on her way out of town and give Lyric a call in a day or so.

Bodhi grabbed the back of his neck and squeezed. He could feel Syn's eyes on him as he walked out of the bar. Her accusing stare and hurt, ate at him. Goddess, he wanted to walk up and take her into his arms. He needed her more than he needed to breathe, but the woman on the other end of the phone needed him more.

"I don't know what to do, Bodhi. I'm scared," she whispered.

He took a deep breath. "I'll head out in the morning Layla. Just hold tight."

"Thank you. Oh, God. I think he's back. I need to go."

Available Now

Accidentally Wolf

Mystic Wolves book 1

"It's okay, little guy," Cora soothed, shoving down her fear for the little wolf caught in the illegal trap. The device had been hidden in a shallow crevice within a couple miles of her veterinary clinic. The way his wound was bleeding she knew, if she didn't get him free, he'd likely die. Inching closer to him, Cora watched for signs of aggression. "I'm going to get you out of there, but you have to promise not to bite me, okay?"

She squatted down until her face was almost level with his. "I'll try not to hurt you."

Cora swore it looked like the little guy nodded. At least Cora hoped that was a nod of agreement. His tiny body shook and shuddered. She prayed she wasn't mistaken.

After carefully looking over the contraption, she realized the jaws were meant for a much larger animal. Luckily for this wolf, his leg wasn't clamped between the steel jaws, only grazed. He was still stuck with his larger paw locked on the inside of the obviously modified bear trap and had a nasty gash that needed tending, sooner rather than later.

What seemed liked hours later, Cora finally got the device forced opened. Sweat trickling down her temples stung her eyes. The wolf lay panting like he'd just ran for miles. His gaze seemed to convey that he trusted her. Although it looked as though the trap only grazed his leg, she still checked to make sure it wasn't broken.

With a glance up at the darkening sky, Cora shrugged out of her jacket, leaving herself in only the yoga leggings and tank top she wore for her daily jog. South Dakota, during the day, could be warm, but as soon as the sun goes down, the temperatures drop dramatically. "Okay, little guy. I'm going to wrap you in my coat, and then I'm going to take you home with me."

Matching actions to words, she gently lifted his body. As she went to place his front right paw inside the jacket, the wolf howled the most pitiful whine, breaking her heart.

"I know it hurts, but I..." Cora jerked back in shock when the wounded animal bit down on her arm.

Once the wolf wriggled out of her coat, Cora watched in amazement as he licked her wound. If she didn't know any better, she'd swear he was apologizing, but thought that would be crazy. She gaped at him and scooted back a step or two, or three, until she stopped herself.

He whined again before trying to stand on his own, falling down when his front leg wouldn't hold him up.

Ignoring her own injury, she grabbed up her jacket and wrapped it around his body, being sure to pay close attention to his bleeding leg. "I know you're hurt, but try not to bite me again." She tried to sound stern when inside she was scared.

The walk back to her clinic took twice as long as normal since she didn't want to jar her patient any more than necessary. Every now and then his rough tongue would peek out and lick her arm. Although she was caught up on all her shots, she still worried about diseases from animals such as the wild wolf. At first glance she thought he was a baby wolf, now with him gathered in her arms and the couple of miles trek back to her home, she discovered he wasn't so young.

"Goodness, you must weigh close to seventy pounds, big guy."

Cora kept up a steady dialogue as she walked. When the clinic came into view, she nearly dropped to her knees in relief. Her arms shook under the stress of holding so much weight for such a long period of time. Normally, the hike would have taken her no time at all, but holding an injured animal that weighed almost as much as she did, the entire way was taxing, to say the least, not to mention the bite on her arm burned like fire.

She stopped outside the back door, adjusting her hold to punch in the code to unlock the back door, and, exhaling in relief, she murmured, "Thank you, technology." Cora's breathing was ragged by the time she made it inside.

Attached to the clinic was her small apartment, with a steel door separating the two spaces. Again, she punched in the code and then used her shoulder to enter the office area.

"Almost there, big guy. I'll have you fixed up in no time." Sweat poured down her chest, soaking her top. Cora ignored it all to focus on getting her patient fixed up. After she'd cleaned his wound, she found he had indeed broken his front leg, which was why he had probably bitten her when she moved him.

Thankful that her training kicked in to tend to the little wolf, when all she wanted to do was curl up in a ball and take a long nap, Cora placed the patched up wolf inside the padded kennel with a sense of relief. He whined when she attempted to lock the gate, his pain-filled gaze breaking her heart.

There were no other patients in the hospital area. She made the decision to leave the lock off, hoping she wasn't making a mistake and headed to take a bath.

Cora wiped her hand across the fogged mirror and stared at her own pain-filled gaze. "How can one little bitty bite hurt so damn much?" She looked at the freshly cleaned wound for what seemed like the thousandth time and stuck a thermometer in her mouth and waited for the beep, promising herself if her temperature was too high, she'd head into town.

Even after taking meds and a cool bath, nothing was bringing her temperature down. Looking at the triple digit reading on the tiny screen she cringed. There was nothing else she could do except head into town to urgent med. Cora really hated to go to the emergency room. She rolled her eyes and shook her head, stopping when the motion made her feel like she was on a tilt-a-whirl.

Wrapping a towel around herself, she decided to check on her patient one more time before she got dressed. The door between her home and the clinic was open, but the lights were out, sending a shiver of fear down her spine. Cora flipped the switch on the wall, illuminating the walkway. Her head felt heavy, the lights overly bright, making her stumble and lose her footing.

"Shit, damn." Rising to her feet, she reached her palm out to the wall to help steady herself and blinked a few times to bring things back into focus.

Standing in the middle of her clinic, with the injured wolf in his hands, was the most magnificent man she'd ever seen in her entire life. At over six foot tall, with short blonde hair and tattoos—lots of tattoos. The man exuded sex and menace. Yes, he definitely looked like he was angry. Even with her head feeling wonky, the sight of the unknown man made her body come alive. A whole different pulse began beating between her thighs, making Cora want to reach out and touch him, and not because she was in fear for her life.

"Who are you, and why do you have my wolf?" Cora was happy her voice didn't come out sounding as scared as she felt.

"Your wolf?"

The big man growled, the sound making her feel things she really shouldn't. Her nipples peaked at his deep rumble. Cora blamed the reaction on the fever.

"Listen, despite the fact you obviously broke into my clinic and I could press charges, I won't, but only if you put the animal down and leave the same way you came. You have less than five minutes, and then my offer is gone." Cora arched an eyebrow at him. "Do we have a deal?"

She waited for him to agree and put the sleeping wolf back down. Instead he quirked an eyebrow of his own, widened his stance, and sniffed the air.

In a move too fast for Cora to comprehend, the hunk standing a good ten feet away from her one moment, was all of a sudden crowding her space, sniffing her neck.

"Hey, have you heard of personal space?" When Cora attempted to push him back, her world spun.

Zayn Malik didn't know whether to laugh or growl at the human who tried to tell him what to do, all while she stood in nothing but a miniscule towel. Holding his nephew in wolf form, he opted for the latter. Every member of their pack knew the rules, and he couldn't imagine Nolan, even at the young age of seven, breaking them. He'd wait until whatever drugs the woman gave Nolan wore off, and his nephew could shift back to find out what happened.

The overwhelming scent of antiseptic clouded his senses, making it hard for him to discern the unusual smells assaulting him. When she raised her hand to push him back, he watched her eyes roll back in her head. Zayn shifted Nolan to one arm, being careful of his injured leg, and caught the woman in his other arm.

That was how his alpha found him, holding an injured cub in one arm and a naked female in the other. It wasn't his fault the towel was dislodged when he pulled her into his arm to stop her from face planting onto the ceramic tile floor.

"You want to tell me why you are holding my cub and an unconscious naked human, Zayn?"

The smile his brother suppressed didn't make Zayn happy. He wanted to toss the human to Niall. Only fear of hurting his nephew kept him from following through on the thought. "Fuck off, Niall," he grumbled.

"Give me Nolan. Do we know what happened to him?" Niall reached for his cub, carefully tucking him into his body.

As he handed Nolan over to Niall, Zayn watched his brother grimace at the bandage on his son's leg, then sniff at the offending thing like he wanted to rip it off. The joking man was gone, replaced by the concerned father. Niall stood at over six foot three with more red in his blonde hair, but with the same blue eyes Zayn had. When Niall spoke as alpha, everyone in the pack listened. Although they had pack mates who were bigger than Niall, none could take him in a fight in human or wolf form.

They'd come to the Mystic River Pack in South Dakota when Niall found his mate by chance during one of their annual bike rides to Sturgis. Within a few months they'd found themselves full-fledged members of the pack, and Niall had learned he was to become a father.

His brother's nose then turned to the woman Zayn cradled in his arms. Niall's face got too close for Zayn's peace of mind to a bandage wrapped around her thin arm, making his inner wolf rumble close to the surface.

"Do you smell that?" Niall sniffed again.

"What?" Zayn pulled the woman closer to his chest, using his large hand to cover as much of her bare ass from his brother as possible.

The right side of Niall's mouth quirked up for a moment before he turned serious. He bent to pick up the towel that had been dropped and draped it over the female.

"She's been bitten."

Narrowing his eyes, Zayn ran his gaze over the sleeping woman. "What did you say?"

The woman in his arms stirred, a feverish light in her eyes. That was when he noticed she was extremely hot to the touch. The smell of the clinic and the medicines had masked the unmistakable scent of the marking, which meant his sweet little nephew had bitten the good doctor when she had obviously tried to help him.

"You smell soooo delicious." Cora licked her lips.

"Um, what's your name, sweetheart?" Zayn tilted his head back from her questing lips and tongue. *Damn, her tongue is really long.*

"Mmm. You taste really good too." Another wet swipe from her tongue had him panting.

"Oh, goddess. Baby, you need to stop." Zayn needed to get the woman to stop licking him or he was going to throw her down on the table and fuck her.

How the hell did she go from being cradled in his arms, to wrapped around him with her legs locked around his hips, and her arms around his head? Zayn swallowed. Jesus, he was ready to come in his jeans with his brother and nephew not five feet away.

"That's enough, Cora." The low timber of Niall's voice reverberated around the room. A shiver went through the woman in his arms, and she swung her stare toward his brother.

Niall held an ID card with a picture of the woman in his arms. The name, Dr. Cora Welch, was at the top for Zayn to see. His brother grinned, his blue eyes dancing with mirth.

Cora's pussy contracted. Holy crap, the man was hot with a capital oh-my-lawd H, and she was humping him like a cat in heat, a naked cat in fricking heat.

She unlocked her ankles from the blonde Adonis's waist, hoping her legs would hold her up. They wobbled but didn't buckle—thankfully. "I'm so sorry...I don't know what came over me."

"I know what almost came all over me."

Sucking in a swift breath, Cora crossed one arm over her breasts and snatched the towel from the red haired man. Not that they hadn't seen everything there was to see, but she was in control of herself now.

"Smooth, Zayn, smooth. I apologize for my brother. He's not usually so crass, but we were worried when we couldn't find our little one here." He indicated the now alert wolf.

Eyes so blue peeked out between the big man's arms, accompanied by the whine she'd become accustomed to from the cub. She reached an unsteady hand toward his head to give a little scratch between his ears.

"Luckily for him, he's going to be okay. I found him stuck in a medieval looking animal trap made for a much larger animal. His little leg here," she indicated his cast, "barely missed being snapped in half by the steel jaws. I set the break and cleaned the wound. He should be right as rain in a few weeks."

Here she was buck-ass naked, carrying on a conversation with two men and a wolf. She was definitely sick. Cora raised her hand to feel her head. The short speech made her breathless, like she'd just run a marathon.

Behind her, she heard something growl. Turning to see the gorgeous man wearing a scowl, she took an involuntary step away. She looked around, fearing a wild animal had somehow gotten inside her office.

"Thank you, Cora Welch, for saving my cub. I owe you a life debt."

She swung her gaze back to the man holding the wolf. "Who are you? I've seen you in town, but I don't think we've met."

"I am Niall Malik. The man behind you is my brother, Zayn Malik."

Cora's tummy fluttered as she looked behind her at the man named Zayn. Lower down, between her thighs, her sex seemed to swell. A woman could come just from the stare of his blue eyed gaze.

"Well, it was very nice to meet you both, but I'm not feeling the best...so, um..."

Cora stumbled forward. A steely arm wrapped around her from behind. Blonde hair lightly dusted the arm roped with muscles upon muscles. Tattoos covered every available inch of skin she could see.

"Easy," Zayn murmured.

Cora blinked. Her stomach twisted; her pulse beat so loud she was sure even the man not holding her could hear it. Why did she feel like something monumental was about to happen?

"What the hell is wrong with me?"

Around her she saw white flashes. More men seemed to fill her once empty clinic. She wasn't a fan of having people witness her in a towel, let alone if she was going to either hump the man holding her or pass out. Either option seemed possible.

She blinked her eyes a few times to clear her vision. The newcomers pushed and jostled or shoved for prime position to see what the action was, making it the last straw for Cora. The equipment, along with all the instruments, was expensive, and not something she wanted to have to replace.

"Everyone stop!" Cora yelled, stepping forward with her hand out, hoping they didn't see the way it shook.

Zayn pulled her in closer to his body, eliminating the small space she'd attempted to put between them for her own peace of mind. Did the man not understand personal space?

Niall inclined his head. "You heard the lady. Everyone move out. The situation is in hand."

"Zayn's got something in hand."

"Watch your tone, McDowell." Niall warned.

McDowell was easily fifty pounds heavier than Niall, and it looked to be all muscle, but he seemed to shrink right before Cora's eyes at Niall's command. Cora studied all the men in front of her with a slow inspection. Faded denim hugged muscular legs, skin tight T-shirts or sleeveless flannel button down covered equally muscular torsos. Each man looked as if he stepped off the cover of some muscle magazine. She may be new to the Mystic River area, but she was pretty sure it was not normal for so many gorgeous men to be in one place, unless...*Oh please don't be gay.*

The extremely large erection digging into her back gave her hope that the man holding her wasn't, but in this day and age one just never knew.

"Sorry, Alpha. We see you found your cub." McDowell nodded towards Niall.

"Yes, let's head back. I'm sure he's tired from his long day."

Cora pulled her attention from checking out the bevy of gorgeous men to see the look of love shining in Niall's eyes as he looked down into the blue eyes of the wolf in his arms.

"Where did you say the trap was, Cora?" Zayn asked.

After she explained where it was located off the running trail, all the men in the room trained their eyes on her. "What are you looking at me like that for?"

"How did you get him back here?" Niall fired the question at her.

"I wrapped him in my jacket, picked him up, and carried him." Her arms still felt like Jell-O from carrying him for over two miles.

"You carried an injured, sixty-five pound cub, over two miles?" Zayn raised his brows.

Cora frowned. "Are you calling me a liar?" She spun out of his arms, nearly falling in her haste. She raised her hand when Zayn reached to touch her. "First of all, he weighs seventy-two pounds." She pointed to the cub in question. "Second of all, I usually run over five miles every day, not to mention I do yoga and cross-fit. So yeah, carrying him was really hard, and I nearly fell several times. My arms hurt just holding them up right now, but I did it, and I would do it again. I am not a liar. You and whoever else who don't believe me can go fuck yourself, and get the hell out of my clinic, because I'm tired, cranky, and I really need to lie down."

"Everybody back the fuck up." Zayn reached for her.

She took a deep breath. There were half a dozen men in the clinic, and she had no clue how they'd gotten in, or why they were all there. "Who are all of you, and why are you here? How did you get in?" The sound of distress from the cub stirred her overprotective instincts.

Forcing herself to turn her attention back to the man who seemed to be in charge, Cora smiled at the wide awake cub. "Did all that ruckus wake you up?"

Cora looked up into blue eyes very similar to the young wolf, but shook off the notion. "He may need some more pain meds. I had him on an IV drip, but *someone* took it out. I can give you some in pill form that you can mix in with his food if you notice him having any discomfort."

"Thank you, Cora. These are men from my...ah...family. When a cub goes missing everyone drops what they're doing to search. I'm sorry if we've scared you." Niall inclined his head.

She flicked away his thank you with a wave of her hand, glad to see almost everyone had cleared out, like they'd been waiting for the order. Now, if she could just get rid of the last of her unwanted visitors, she could go to bed. Surely by the time she woke up in the morning, she'd feel much better. If not, she'd go to the doctor, even if she hated the thought of that.

"Do you have someone to take care of you?" Niall asked.

"I don't need anyone taking care of me."

"I'm afraid I can't leave you here alone, Cora. Either you come home with us, or Zayn stays with you. We owe you a life debt."

"That's...that's crazy. I just saved your pet. Now you have him and everything is fine. I just have a bit of a cold. It's fine."

Niall shook his head, and Zayn's scowl deepened. "Seriously, I'm fine," she repeated.

"You coming with us, or is he staying here?"

He was an immovable obstacle. What do you do with an immovable obstacle? You go around him. Cora was glad her wits were still functioning, even though she knew her fever had to be even higher than the last time she took it.

"How about if I take some meds and call you in the morning?" See, she could be reasonable. She nodded.

"Did you grab her bag?"

With a quick glance, Cora gawked at the sight of Zayn holding her overnight bag with more than just a change of clothing. "Yes," Zayn growled.

"Good. Grab the girl."

What were the chances she could make it down the hall to her apartment with the steel door before either man could catch her? And if she did make it, could she get the alarm set and the police called before she passed out?

All these questions became a moot point when the man in front of her turned on his bare feet, which she just noticed, and walked out the front door, while Zayn murmured next to her ear, "You wouldn't make it two feet before I caught you."

"What?" Her voice came out in a breathless squeak she blamed on fright.

"You have very expressive eyes, and they were saying very clearly that you were about to do a runner. Rest assured, nobody, and I mean nobody in our...home would ever hurt you. We only want to see to your safety and wellbeing."

The last bit of strength Cora possessed left her all at once. Fortunately for her, Zayn just happened to be there to stop her from kissing the floor. Still, common sense told her she should let someone know where she was, just in case they planned to murder her—or something.

"I need to let my assistant know where I am in case of an emergency."

"It's Saturday. Aren't you closed on Sundays?"

Her challenge almost faded on her lips, not because she'd lost her senses, but because he'd bent his head so close to hers she could feel his breath on her lips. For a moment she almost forgot how to breathe. Holy buckets, the man was potent.

"I said in case of an emergency."

"Fine. Who do you need to call?"

Cora swallowed. Surely if they were going to kill her, they wouldn't allow her to let people know where she was going. Right?

With a grunt, Zayn waited while she left a voicemail for her assistant, letting her know she'd be staying with the Maliks and to call her cell if she needed her.

"Okay. You can put me down."

"Not gonna happen. You'll fall down, and then Niall will blame me."

Cora gaped at his audacity. "You can't carry me all the way back to your place."

"One of the guys brought my truck. I only have to carry you out front," he grunted.

She was too tired, and honestly too sick, to argue any further. Besides, his shoulder really felt good to lay her head on. "You smell really, really good."

"You said that before."

Cora closed her eyes against the flashes of white light.

Zayn pulled the door closed, engaging the locks. "Any problems on your way back, Kellen?"

"Coast was clear. Everything okay on your end, boss?" Kellen called from his place against the wall of the clinic.

At the sound of the newcomer's voice, Cora turned her head into Zayn's chest.

"Yes. Thank you for bringing my rig. Can you drive while I hold her? I don't think she will let me go long enough to let me drive us home."

She really wanted to lift her head and give him the finger, but at that very minute she couldn't. The steady rocking from his walk was so soothing her body went lax. Instead of fighting sleep, she let it claim her. A sense of security wrapped around her in the tattooed arms of the big man that she hadn't felt in a long time.

FireStarter
SmokeJumpers Book 1

Keanu Raine walked a few feet from his team, letting his inner fire control him. The forest fire was all but burned out, but it was searching for more, and he knew it had found a new source. The living, breathing entity of unforgiving heat that could engulf hundreds of acres only needed a little spark to ignite all over again, only Keanu wasn't going to allow it if he could stop it. He ignored their questions knowing they were missing something. The hair on the back of his neck stood on end, never a good sign when you were in the middle of a huge forest fire. "Hey, did you guys hear that?" Keanu asked.

"Shit, man, this gobbler is a fuck nut," Brax McKay grumbled.

"Kea, all I can hear is my stomach rumbling." Hal Aldridge grinned, his blond hair soaked with sweat.

"I swear something's not right." Keanu nodded in the direction of the burned out forest.

He couldn't squash the feeling of doom as he looked through the smoke. His inner fire leapt to life, sending his senses on high alert. A small blaze could easily turn into something much larger with the dry conditions, and in Keanu's opinion, it was a guarantee. They'd evacuated the surrounding homes, but it wasn't always a certainty all families would get out.

"I'm going to scout around a bit, since we have about thirty minutes before pick-up. You guys head for the zone and wait for my call. If I'm not there when the DC shows, I'll meet you at the next drop." He tapped the radio attached to his suit.

"Yeah, right, boss. I don't think so, I'm going with you," Hal snorted, moving to stand by him.

"It's cool. I'll go by myself. It's probably nothing." Keanu shrugged.

Hal shook his head. "Let's go."

The group of smokejumpers paused and Keanu nodded to Brax. He knew Hal would follow him regardless. They left the other six members of their team and headed in the direction that Keanu sensed the disturbance. The overwhelming feeling persisted. Someone was trapped in the middle of the blaze. He could feel it in his bones. They needed to locate him or her quickly, or there wouldn't be anything left to find.

Several minutes later, they stood on the outskirts of an already evacuated community. Keanu considered calling a stop to their search, fearing he was too late. There were towering homes to his right, less than a hundred yards away, and blackened earth to his left.

"Kea, if there was someone here, they must've gotten out."

Keanu wasn't sure how Hal knew he was searching for a person, but he had figured out early on Hal was every bit as sensitive as he was.

Hearing Hal mimic his thoughts about their search made his stomach drop. The other man didn't have to add *or they were dead*; nothing could've survived in the middle of the area.

Keanu shook his head, not willing to give up yet. "This way, I know I'm right." Turning toward the trees, he didn't need to check to see if his partner followed.

Burnt wood and grass surrounded them. Inhaling deeply he caught a scent so distinctive it made most people gag.

"My water tank is almost empty. If there's a fire, and I'm not saying there is, maybe we should call for back-up."

"There isn't time. I smell burnt human hair." "Shit," Hal swore.

Keanu led them into a thick clump of charred trees. With all the blackness surrounding him, he couldn't see a thing, but he sensed a hot spot. A tingling deep inside wouldn't let him ignore what he knew was a real threat. He rushed to the area before coming to an abrupt halt. A large section of land filled with tall dry grass had started to smolder.

"What the fuck? How the hell did we miss this?" Hal pointed. "Look." A small boy was nestled in the branches just above the flames.

"Hal, you climb and I'll take care of the fire," Keanu ordered, relieved to see his partner and best friend didn't argue for once.

Stepping over the fallen branches and blackened areas, he inhaled the hot air into his lungs. He continued sucking the flames into his body, relishing the feel of the warmth rushing through his system, while using the water hose attached to his pack to douse the hot spots.

By the time Hal had the boy on the ground, he couldn't sense any more flames. He coughed and gave Hal two thumbs up.

They made their way back to their teammates with the small boy cradled in Hal's big arms.

"What the hell?" Brax eyed the child.

Keanu grabbed a bottle of water from his coworker and chugged, while the rest of the group tended to the boy. His inner flame began to cool with the refreshing fluid and he accepted another bottle gratefully.

"Oh man, Kea. You saved the boy's life." Barry looked from the boy to Keanu. Keanu shook his head. "Nah, I just got lucky. Hal got the kid down." "Bullshit! Good job, Kea." Brax punched his arm.

Praise from his team made Keanu cringe. None of them were ordinary men, far from it, but he hated having attention drawn to him. He looked to the sky, happy to see their pick-up overhead in time to save him from unwanted admiration. They'd radioed ahead, alerting them to the addition. The first man took the child. Keanu was the last to leave the clearing. Giving his inner fire free reign one last time, he made sure they hadn't missed anything else. By the time they finished, he was sure the next team wouldn't have any surprises.

Getting into the DC-3 wasn't nearly as fun as jumping from one, Keanu mused as he was finally lifted up.

Keanu stood on his deck gazing at the openness for as far as his eyes could see. He loved the smell of the mountains, the clean pine scent. It was very similar to his home with his grandparents. He raised his face to the sun, allowing the rays to warm him from the outside as his internal fire warmed the inside. Letting out a deep breath, he turned toward the fire pit in the corner and blew a puff of air on the logs, making them burn.

Smiling, Keanu stepped into his spacious kitchen and grabbed a bottle of beer from the fridge. Closing his eyes in bliss as he twisted off the cap, he tipped his head for a much needed drink. A platter of steaks and two potatoes wrapped in foil were on the counter, ready to be cooked. He grabbed the platter, stepped outside and placed them on the grill, then with another breath of air, the charcoals started to smoke and turn a fiery red.

"Yo, Kea. Where you at?" Hal yelled from inside.

"I'm on the deck. Grab a beer and come on out."

Hal ducked his head, avoiding the doorjamb, and joined Keanu on the deck with two bottles dangling from his fingers. Keanu took a bottle from Hal with a shake of his head.

"Oofta, I so needed this." Hal tipped his bottle to his mouth.

Keanu laughed and flipped the steaks. "Is 'oofta' a real word?"

"Hell yeah, it's real. You can use it for just about any swear word."

Keanu stifled a chuckle. "Thanks, but I think I'll just say 'fuck' at least once in every sentence."

"Why doesn't that surprise me?" "Fuck off." Keanu laughed.

They sat in companionable silence, listening to the birds sing and the wind whistle through the trees. Keanu loved being outside almost as much as he loved women. He swore watching the trees sway was like watching a woman sashay as she led her man to bed.

"So, what did your grandfather want?"

Leave it to Hal to cut to the chase before Keanu was ready to talk about it. His grandfather lived at the top of the Cascades. It was only fifty miles away, but it could be another country.

Keanu shrugged. "Something is spooking him, and if you knew my grandfather, you'd know it was major. He scares the shit out of me and I'm a grown man."

"He didn't give you any hints?"

Keanu looked at the pit and sucked in a breath, making the red coals lose some of their glow, before turning to his best friend. "Nah. He needs my *expertise*." Keanu made air quotes, shrugged, and headed to the grill.

"So, are you looking forward to going home, boss?" Hal asked.

"Yes and no."

"We're going to miss you on the team. Not sure what we'll do without our very own fireman." Hal laughed, his booming voice echoing in the still of the night.

"Real funny. I'm still on call in case of emergency situations, and you know Brax can bend things to his will." Keanu raised his eyebrows. The co-leader of their group had truly amazing and sometimes frightening powers, but Keanu wasn't going to tell him he thought he was great.

The man already had a big head.

Keanu flipped the steaks and checked the potatoes.

"I'm going to miss my own personal barbeque-man." Hal had a frown on his face.

He flipped Hal off. He'd had the ability to make a fire out of air since he was a small boy. By the time he'd turned twelve, he'd learned to breathe the fire back into his body without much cost to himself, other than the need to burn off the energy one way or another.

After graduating from high school he became a fireman for the local fire department. Known as a fire-breather in the world of elementals, Keanu could create a small flame or a large roaring blaze, and in the next breath suck it back into his body. Of course, the larger the fire the more energy he needed to burn afterwards.

As a child, he'd hike for miles and freefall off a cliff into the freezing streams surrounding the Cascades. The adult Keanu found other more pleasurable ways to expel the effects, usually between the thighs of a woman.

"You need some help there, Kea?"

Keanu shook off his thoughts of the past. "Could you grab the salad and dressing out of the fridge?"

"No problem."

Within moments, Keanu had the steaks and potatoes on the table. It always amazed him the way the six foot four blond giant waited until everything was set before digging into his food. He'd slice his steak with exact precision into small cube-like bites, and then stab them with his fork, before chewing each piece several times.

Hal always consumed the meat first, then the carbs, followed by whatever was left, claiming he liked to eat the good stuff first. It amused Keanu to watch him. Being a man who loved his sweets, Keanu would skip the meal and eat dessert first when he could.

"Why are you staring at me like I'm some kind of lab experiment?" Hal asked.

Keanu shook his head, raised his fork and pointed it at his friend. "You are the weirdest eater."

Hal raised his bottle. "I get no complaints from the ladies."

"Thanks for the visual, dude."

Ankles crossed, hands resting over his full belly, Keanu leaned his head on the back of his chair and stared at the darkening sky.

Hal kicked Keanu's feet on the ottoman. With a grunt, Keanu made room for the other man to stretch out his long legs, too.

"Have you ever had the feeling your world was about to get rocked?" Keanu asked without looking at Hal.

"Yep! Every time I take a lady to bed." Hal wagged his eyebrows.

"Shut up, dick," he laughed. "I don't mean like that. Besides, I don't get my world rocked when I fuck a woman, I rock *her* world." Keanu smirked.

"Man, you're so full of it. I heard Cathy calling you all kinds of names and none of them good." Hal punched Keanu's arm.

"Damn, she's one crazy-ass bitch. Seriously though, have you ever gotten a feeling nothing is gonna be the same again?" Keanu brought the conversation back around, avoiding the unwanted reminder of his ex.

Hal bumped his size fourteen feet against Keanu's before answering. He felt like a pussy for voicing his fears.

"I don't discount any mysterious crap. For real, my grandmother used to talk about the berserkers in my family, and how they came back every hundred years or some shit. I'm the first *blond giant* in over ten decades." He gave Keanu a pointed look. "My Nana's words, not mine. Sometimes, when I'm in the middle of a fire, I feel like another person is in my body. Ya know what I mean?" Color spread across Hal's face.

Keanu knew exactly what he meant. Every member of their Smokejumper group had special abilities. Hal was clearly a human wrecking ball. He just hadn't realized Hal wasn't always in control, or didn't feel like it at least. "I think we all feel like that to an extent. Have you talked to the captain about it?"

Hal pinned him with a look brooking no argument. "Nothing to talk about."

They fell silent. Keanu let the quiet of the night soothe his soul. One of the reasons he and Hal were such good friends was because neither man pried into the other's business.

"I'd better get going. You want me to help clean up?" Hal nodded at the dishes on the table.

"Nah, I got it."

"Hey, I owe you for cooking, but I haven't mastered the art of making anything other than

Ramen noodles yet."

Keanu blinked his eyes. "Because you have the poor little boy look down to an art. You bat those baby blues and all the ladies line up to cook for you."

"Well, you just smile that bright cheesy-ass grin and the ladies are lining up to take their panties off for you. I think that trumps my free meals."

Both men laughed at the familiar argument, since neither man lacked for food or companionship.

They were opposite in looks. Keanu had dark hair hanging past his shoulders, dark brown eyes, and topped out at six foot. Hal was built more like a swimmer, and had at least three inches on him. Keanu had the physique of a body builder and spent his off-time working out or participating in extreme sports.

Brax, the co-leader of his team of Smokejumpers, recruited Keanu at twenty-two when he'd made national headlines. Now at thirty-three, he was ready to head home and settle down. Being seven years older than Hal, he considered him like a little brother. As the unofficial leader of the team it was his job to watch over the guys, but he'd taken Hal under his wing. Knowing he'd possibly done his last jump, and he and Hal would no longer be working together, Keanu already missed his friend.

He walked Hal to the door and watched as the big man took the stairs two at a time, before jumping into his oversized four-wheel-drive pickup. Hal waved one big hand out the window before executing a U-turn to leave. Keanu waited until the taillights disappeared down the long drive before going inside. After cleaning up the mess, he shed his clothes and stood under the rainforest-like shower he'd installed on his deck. Sighing, he closed his eyes.

About Elle Boon

Elle Boon lives in Middle-Merica as she likes to say...with her husband, two kids, and a black lab who is more like a small pony. She'd never planned to be a writer, but when life threw her a curve, she swerved with it, since she's athletically challenged. She's known for saying "Bless Your Heart" and dropping lots of F-bombs, but she loves where this new journey has taken her.

She writes what she loves to read, and that is romance, whether it's erotic or paranormal, as long as there is a happily ever after. Her biggest hope is that after readers have read one of her stories, they fall in love with her characters as much as she did. She loves creating new worlds and has more stories just waiting to be written. Elle believes in happily ever afters, and can guarantee you will always get one with her stories.

Connect with Elle online, she loves to hear from you:

www.elleboon.com

https://www.facebook.com/elle.boon

https://www.facebook.com/pages/Elle-Boon-Author/1429718517289545

https://twitter.com/ElleBoon1

https://www.facebook.com/groups/1405756769719931/

https://www.facebook.com/groups/wewroteyourbookboyfriends/

https://www.goodreads.com/author/show/8120085.Elle_Boon

www.elleboon.com/newsletter

Other Books By Elle Boon

Erotic Ménage
Ravens of War
Selena's Men
Two For Tamara
Jaklyn's Saviors
Kira's Warriors
Shifters Romance
Mystic Wolves
Accidentally Wolf
His Perfect Wolf
Jett's Wild Wolf
Paranormal Romance
SmokeJumpers
FireStarter
Berserker's Rage
A SmokeJumpers Christmas
Mind Bender, Coming Soon
MC Shifters Erotic
Iron Wolves MC
Lyric's Accidental Mate
Xan's Feisty Mate
Kellen's Tempting Mate
Slater's Enchanting Mate
Dark Lovers
Bodhi's Synful Mate
Contemporary Romance
Miami Nights

Miami Inferno
Rescuing Miami, Coming 2017
Miami Blaze, Coming 2017
SEAL Team Phantom Series
Delta Salvation
Delta Recon
Delta Rogue
Mission Saving Shayna, Omega Team
Protecting Teagan, SEAL of Protection
WILD AND DIRTY, A Wild Irish Novella, Coming April
2017

11-18

DISCARD

CPSIA information can be obtained
at www.ICGtesting.com
Printed in the USA
LVHW011451301018
595357LV00010B/692/P

9 781543 053647